SOMETHING
FROM THE
NIGHTSIDE

SIMON R. GREEN

2003
50TH
ANNIVERSARY

ACE BOOKS, NEW YORK

SOMETHING FROM THE NIGHTSIDE

An Ace Book / published by arrangement with
the author

PRINTING HISTORY
Ace mass-market edition / June 2003

Copyright © 2003 by Simon R. Green.
Cover art by Jonathan Barkat.
Cover design by Judy Murello.
Text design by Julie Rogers.

ISBN: 978-0-441-01065-3

ACE®
Ace Books are published by The Berkley Publishing Group,
a division of Penguin Group (USA) Inc.,
375 Hudson Street, New York, New York 10014.
ACE and the "A" design
are trademarks belonging to Penguin Group (USA) Inc.

PRINTED IN THE UNITED STATES OF AMERICA

20   19   18   17   16   15   14   13

continued . . .

"What makes this novel stand out among its numerous peers is the lead characters whose love and commitment to one another in the midst of epic escapades keeps them grounded in humanity." —*Midwest Book Review*

Blue Moon Rising

"Mr. Green turns quite a few fantasy cliches delightfully topsy-turvy in this wry, sometimes caustic narrative. The well-orchestrated plot features a bevy of fascinating characters, whose behavior varies from whimsical eccentricity to that of intense emotional motivation. This fantasy adventure is one readers will savor and enjoy for a long time to come."

—*Rave Reviews*

"Really stands out from the crowd. Breathes new life into an old story." —*Science Fiction Chronicle*

The Adventures of Hawk & Fisher

"Intrigue and magic . . . an interesting and well-conceived blend." —*Science Fiction Chronicle*

"Good fun." —*Asimov's Science Fiction*

I went to a house that was not a house.
I opened a door that was not a door.
And what I saw, I saw.

ONE

Money Comes Walking In

Private eyes come in all shapes and sizes, and none of them look like television stars. Some do insurance work, some hang around cheap hotels with camcorders hoping to get evidence for divorce cases, and damn few ever get to investigate complicated murder mysteries. Some chase things that don't exist, or shouldn't. Me, I find things. Sometimes I'd rather not find them, but that comes with the territory.

The flaking sign on the door in those days said *Taylor Investigations*. I'm Taylor. Tall, dark and not particularly handsome. I bear the scars of old cases proudly, and I never let down a client. Provided they've paid at least some cash up front.

My office back then was cosy, if you were feeling charitable, cramped if you weren't. I spent a lot of time there. It beat having a life. It was a low-rent office in a low-rent area. All the businesses with any sense were moving out, making more room for those of us who operated in the greyer areas of the legal and illegal. Even the rats were just passing through, on their way to somewhere more civilised. My neighbours were a dentist and an accountant, both of them struck off, both of whom made more money than I did.

It was raining hard the night Joanna Barrett came to see me. The kind of cold, driving, pitiless rain that makes you glad to be safe and dry indoors. I should have taken that as an omen, but I've never been very good at picking up on hints. It was late, well past the point where the day starts edging into evening, and everyone else in the building had gone home. I was still sitting behind my desk, half-watching the portable television with its sound turned down, while the man on the phone yelled in my ear. He wanted money, the fool. I made sympathetic noises in all the right places, waiting for him to get tired and go away, and then my ears pricked up as I heard footsteps in the hall outside, heading for my door. Steady, unhurried . . . and a woman. Interesting. Women always make the best clients. They say they want information, but mostly what they really want is revenge; and they aren't mean when it comes to paying for what they want. What they need. Hell hath no fury; and I should know.

The footsteps stopped outside my door, and a tall shadow studied the bullet hole in the frosted-glass window. I really should have got that seen to, but it made such a great conversation piece. Clients like a touch of romance and danger when they're hiring a private detective, even if they only want some papers served. The door opened, and she walked in. A tall good-looking blonde who reeked of money and class, looking immediately out of place amid the battered furniture and cracked-plaster walls of my office.

Her clothes had the quiet elegance and style that shrieks of serious money, and when she spoke my name her voice had an aristocratic edge that could cut glass. Either she'd been to all the very best boarding and finishing schools, or she'd spent a hell of a lot on elocution lessons. She was perhaps a little too slender, with a raw-boned face and minimal make-up that meant she would always be handsome rather than pretty. From the way she stood, the way she held herself, it was obvious she was a control freak, and the set of her perfectly made-up mouth showed she was used to being obeyed. I notice things like that. It's my job. I gave her my best unimpressed nod and gestured for her to take a seat on the only other chair, on the opposite side of my desk. She sat down without taking out a handkerchief to clean the seat first, and I gave her extra points for bravery. I watched her look around my office, while the voice in the phone at my ear grew ever more hysterical, demanding money with menaces. Very specific menaces. Her face was studiously calm, even blank, but as I glanced around my office, it was only too easy to see it as she saw it.

A battered desk, with only a few token papers in the in and out trays, a fourth-hand filing cabinet, and a rickety couch pushed back against the wall. Rumpled blankets and a dented pillow on the couch showed someone had been sleeping on it regularly. The single window behind my desk had bars on the outside, and the glass rattled loosely in its frame as the wind goosed it. The scuffed carpet had holes, the portable television on my desk was black and white, and the only note of colour on my walls was a give-away girlie calendar. Old delivery pizza boxes stood stacked in one corner. It didn't take a genius to work out this wasn't just an office. Someone lived here. It was also patently obvious that this wasn't the office of someone on his way up.

I'd chosen to live in the real world, for what seemed like good reasons at the time, but it had never been easy.

I suddenly decided I'd had enough of the voice on the telephone. "Look," I said, in that calm reasonable tone that if done properly can drive people absolutely batshit, "if I had the money I'd pay you, but I don't have the money. So you'll just have to take a number and get in line. You are of course welcome to try sueing, in which case I can recommend a neighbour of mine who's a lawyer. He needs the work, so he won't laugh in your face when you tell him who you're trying to get money out of. However, if you'd care to be patient just a little longer, it's possible a whole lot of money just walked in . . . You know, hysteria like that can't be good for your blood pressure. I recommend deep breathing and visits to the seaside. I always find the sea very soothing. I'll get back to you. Eventually."

I put the phone down firmly and smiled politely at my visitor. She didn't smile back. I just knew we were going to get along. She looked pointedly at the murmuring television on my desk, and I turned it off.

"It's company," I said calmly. "Much like a dog, but with the added advantage that you don't have to take it for walks."

"Don't you ever go home?" Her tone made it clear she was asking for information, not because she cared.

"I am currently in between homes. Big, empty, expensive things. Besides, I like it here. Everything's within reach, and nobody bothers me when the day's over. Usually."

"I know it's late. I didn't want to be seen coming here."

"I can understand that."

She sniffed briefly. "You have a hole in your office door, Mr. Taylor."

I nodded. "Moths."

The corners of her dark red mouth turned down, and for a moment I thought she was going to get up and leave. I have that effect on people. But she controlled herself and gave me her best intimidating glare.

"I'm Joanna Barrett."

I nodded, non-commitally. "You say that like it should mean something to me."

"To anyone else, it would," she said, just a little acidly. "But then, I don't suppose you read the business pages, do you?"

"Not unless someone pays me to. Am I to take it you're rich?"

"Extremely."

I grinned. "The very best kind of client. What can I do for you?"

She shifted slightly in her chair, clutching her oversized white leather handbag protectively to her. She didn't want to be here, talking to the likes of me. No doubt usually she had people to take care of such unpleasant tasks for her. But something was eating at her. Something personal. Something she couldn't trust to anyone else. She needed me. I could tell. Hell, I was already counting the money.

"I have need of a private investigator," she said abruptly. "You were . . . recommended to me."

I nodded, understandingly. "Then you've already tried the police, and all the big private agencies, and none of them were able to help you. Which means your problem isn't one of the usual ones."

She nodded stiffly. "They let me down. All of them. Took my money and gave me nothing but excuses. Bastards. So I called in every favour I was owed, pulled every string I had, and eventually someone gave me your name. I understand you find people."

"I can find anyone or anything, if the price is right. It's a gift. I'm dogged and determined and a whole bunch of other things that begin with *d*, and I never give up as long as the cheques keep coming. But, I don't do insurance work, I don't do divorces, and I don't solve crimes. Hell, I wouldn't know a clue if I fell over it. I just find things. Whether they want to be found or not."

Joanna Barrett gave me her best icy disapproving look. "I don't like being lectured."

I smiled easily. "All part of the service."

"And I don't care for your attitude."

"Not many do."

She seriously considered leaving again. I watched her struggle with herself, my face calm and relaxed. Someone like her wouldn't have come this far unless she was really desperate.

"My daughter is . . . missing," she said finally, reluctantly. "I want you to find her for me."

She produced an eight-by-ten glossy photo from her oversized bag, and skimmed it across the table towards me with an angry flick of her hand. I studied the photo without touching it. A head and shoulders shot of a scowling teenager stared sullenly back at me, narrowed eyes peering past a rat's nest of long blonde hair. She would have been pretty if she hadn't been frowning so hard. She looked like she had a mad on for the whole damned world, and it would have been a sucker who bet on the world. In other words, every inch her mother's daughter.

"Her name is Catherine, Mr. Taylor." Joanna Barrett's voice was suddenly quieter, more subdued. "Only answers to Cathy, when she answers at all. She's fifteen, going on sixteen, and I want her found."

I nodded. We were on familiar territory so far. "How long has she been gone?"

"Just over a month." She paused, and then added reluctantly, "This time."

I nodded again. It helps me look thoughtful. "Anything happen recently to upset your daughter?"

"There was an argument. Nothing we haven't said before, God knows. I don't know why she runs away. She's had everything she ever wanted. Everything."

She dug in her bag again and came out with cigarettes and lighter. The cigarettes were French, the lighter was gold with a monogram. I raised my rates accordingly. She lit a cigarette with a steady hand,

and then scattered nervous little puffs of smoke across my office. People shouldn't smoke in situations like this. It's far too revealing. I pushed across my single ash-tray, the one shaped like a lung, and studied the photo again. I wasn't immediately worried about Cathy Barrett. She looked like she could take care of herself, and anybody else stupid enough to bother her. I decided it was time to start asking some obvious questions.

"How about Catherine's father? How does your daughter get on with him?"

"She doesn't. He walked out on us when she was two. Only decent thing the selfish bastard ever did for us. His lawyers got him access, but he hardly ever takes advantage of it. I still have to chase him for maintenance money. Not that we need it, of course, but it's the principle of the thing. And before you ask, no; there's never been any problems with drugs, alcohol, money, or unsuitable boyfriends. I've seen to that. I've always protected her, and I've never once raised a hand to her. She's just a sullen, ungrateful little bitch."

For a moment something glistened in her eyes that might have been tears, but the moment passed. I leaned back in my chair, as though considering what I'd been told, but it all looked pretty straight forward to me. Tracking a runaway wasn't much of a case, but as it happened I was short on cases and cash, and there were bills that need paying. Urgently. It hadn't been a good year—not for a long time. I leaned forward, resting my elbows in my desk, putting on my serious, committed face.

"So, Mrs. Barrett, essentially what we have here is a poor little rich girl who thinks she has everything but love. Probably begging for spare change down in the Underground, eating left-overs and stale bread, sleeping on park benches; hanging out with all the wrong sorts and kidding herself it's all one big adventure. Living life in the raw, with the real people. Secure in the knowledge that once again she's managed to secure her mother's full attention. I wouldn't worry about her too much. She'll come home, once it starts getting cold at nights."

Joanna Barrett was already shaking her expensively coiffured head. "Not this time. I've had experienced people looking for her for weeks now, and no-one's been able to find a trace of her. None of her previous . . . associates have seen anything of her, even with the more than generous rewards I've been offering. It's as though she's vanished off the face of the earth. I've always been able to locate her before. My people have contacts everywhere. But this time, all I have for my efforts is a name I don't recognise. A name, given to me by the same person who supplied me with your name. He said I'd find my daughter . . . in the Nightside."

A cold hand clutched at my heart as I sat up straight. I should have known. I should have known the past never leaves you alone, no matter how far you run from it. I looked her straight in the eye. "What do you know about the Nightside?"

She didn't flinch, but she looked like she wanted to. I can sound dangerous when I have to. She covered her lapse by grinding out her half-finished cigarette in my ash-tray, concentrating on doing the job properly so she wouldn't have to look at me for a while.

"Nothing," she said finally. "Not a damned thing. I'd never heard the name before, and the few of my people who recognised it . . . wouldn't talk to me about it. When I pressed them, they quit, just walked out on me. Walked away from more money than they'd ever made in their life before, rather than discuss the Nightside. They looked at me as though I was . . . sick, just for wanting to discuss it."

"I'm not surprised." My voice was calm again, though still serious, and she looked at me again. I chose my words carefully. "The Nightside is the secret, hidden, dark heart of the city. London's evil twin. It's where the really wild things are. If your daughter's found her way there, she's in real trouble."

"That's why I've come to you," said Joanna. "I understand you operate in the Nightside."

"No. Not for a long time. I ran away, and I vowed I'd never go back. It's a bad place."

She smiled, back on familiar ground again. "I'm

prepared to be very generous, Mr. Taylor. How much do you want?"

I considered the matter. How much, to go back into the Nightside? How much is your soul worth? Your sanity? Your self-respect? But work had been hard to come by for some time now, and I needed the money. There were bad people in this part of London too, and I owed some of them a lot more than was healthy. I considered the matter. Shouldn't be that difficult, finding a teenage runaway. A quick in-and-out job. Probably in and gone before anyone even knew I was there. If I was lucky. I looked at Joanna Barrett and doubled what I had been going to ask her.

"I charge a grand a day, plus expenses."

"That's a lot of money," she said, automatically.

"How much is your daughter worth?"

She nodded briskly, acknowledging the point. She didn't really care what I charged. People like me would always be chump change to people like her.

"Find my daughter, Mr. Taylor. Whatever it takes."

"No problem."

"And bring her back to me."

"If that's what she wants. I won't drag her home against her will. I'm not in the kidnapping business."

It was her turn to lean forward now. Her turn to try and look dangerous. Her gaze was flat and hard, and her words could have been chipped out of ice.

"When you take my money, you do as I say. You

find that spoilt little cow, you drag her out of whatever mess she's got herself into this time, and you bring her home to me. Then, and only then, will you get paid. Is that clear?"

I just sat there and smiled at her, entirely unimpressed. I'd seen a lot scarier than her, in my time. And compared to what was waiting for me back in the Nightside, her anger and implied threats were nothing. Besides, I was her last chance, and both of us knew it. No-one ever comes to me first, and it had nothing to do with what I charge. I have an earned reputation for doing things my own way, for tracking down the truth whatever it takes, and to hell with whoever gets hurt in the process. Including, sometimes, my clients. They always say they want the truth, the whole truth and nothing but the truth, but few of them really mean it. Not when a little white lie can be so much more comforting. But I don't deal in lies. Which is why I've never made the kind of money that would allow me to move in Mrs. Barrett's circles. People only come to me when they've tried absolutely everything else, including prayer and fortune-tellers. There was no-one else left for Joanna Barrett to turn to. She tried to stare me down for a while, and couldn't. She seemed to find that reassuring. She rummaged in her bag again, took out a completed cheque, and tossed it onto my desk. Apparently it was time for plan B.

"Fifty thousand pounds, Mr. Taylor. There will be another cheque just like it, when this is all over."

I kept a straight face, but inside I was grinning broadly. For a hundred grand, I'd find the crew of the *Marie Celeste*. It almost made going back into the Nightside worthwhile. Almost.

"There is . . . a condition."

I smiled. "I thought there might be."

"I'm going with you."

I sat up straight again. "No. No way. No way in Hell."

"Mr. Taylor . . ."

"You don't know what you're asking . . ."

"She's been gone over a month! She's never been gone this long before. Anything could have happened to her by now. I have to be there . . . when you find her."

I shook my head, but I already knew I was going to lose this one. I've always been a soft touch where family is concerned. It's what comes of never having known one. Joanna still wouldn't cry, but her eyes were bright and shining, and for the first time her voice was unsteady.

"Please." She didn't look comfortable saying the word, but she said it anyway. Not for herself, but for her daughter. "I have to come with you. I have to know. I can't just sit at home any more, waiting for the phone to ring. You know the Nightside. Take me there."

We stared at each other for a while, both of us perhaps seeing a little more of the other than we were used to showing the world. And in the end I nodded, as we both knew I would. But for her sake, I tried one more time to make her see reason.

"Let me tell you about the Nightside, Joanna. They call London the Smoke, and everyone knows there's no smoke without fire. The Nightside is a square mile of narrow streets and back alleys in the centre of city, linking slums and tenements that were old when the last century was new. That's if you believe the official maps. In practice, the Nightside is much bigger than that, as though space itself has reluctantly expanded to fit in all the darkness and evil and generally strange stuff that has set up home there. There are those who say the Nightside is actually bigger than the city that surrounds it, these days. Which says something very disturbing about human nature and appetites, if you think about it. Not to mention inhuman appetites. The Nightside has always been a cosmopolitan kind of place.

"It's always night in the Nightside. It's always three o'clock in the morning, and the dawn never comes. People are always coming and going, drawn by needs that dare not speak their names, searching for pleasures and services unforgivable in the sane, daylight world. You can buy or sell anything in the Nightside, and no-one asks questions. No-one cares. There's a nightclub, where you can pay to see a fallen angel forever burning inside a pentacle drawn in baby's blood. Or a decapitated goat's head, that can tell the future in enigmatic verses of perfect iambic pentameter. There's a room where silence is caged, and colours are forbidden, and another where a dead nun will show you her stigmata, for the right price. She didn't rise again, after all, but she'll still let you stick your fingers in the blood-caked holes, if you want.

"Everything you ever feared or dreamed of is running loose somewhere in the shifting streets of the Nightside, or waiting patiently for you in the expensive private rooms of patrons-only clubs. You can find anything in the Nightside, if it doesn't find you first. It's a sick, magical, dangerous place. You still want to go there?"

"You're lecturing me again."

"Answer the question."

"How could such a place exist, right here in the heart of London, without everyone knowing?"

"It exists because it has always existed, and it stays a secret because the powers that be, the real powers, want it that way. You could die there. I could die there, and I know my way around. Or at least, I did. I haven't been back in years. Still want to do this?"

"I'll go wherever my daughter is," Joanna said firmly. "We haven't always been . . . as close as I would have liked, but I'll go into Hell itself to get her back."

I smiled at her then, and there was little humour in that smile. "You may have to, Joanna. You might very well have to."

TWO

Getting There

My name is John Taylor. Everyone in the Nightside knows that name.

I'd been living an ordinary life in the ordinary world, and as a reward no-one had tried to kill me in ages. I liked being anonymous. It took the pressure off. The pressure of recognition, of expectations and destiny. And no; I don't feel like explaining any of that just yet. I hit thirty a few months ago, but found it hard to give a damn. When you've been through as much bad fortune as I have in my time, you learn not to sweat the small stuff. But even the small problems of an everyday world can mount up, and so there I was, going back again, back to the Nightside, despite all my better judgment. I left the Nightside five years ago, fleeing imminent death and the betrayal of friends, and swore through blood-flecked lips that I'd never go back, no matter what. I should have re-membered; God does so love to make a man break a promise.

God, or Someone.

I was going back to a place where everyone knew me, or thought they did. I could have been a con-tender, if I'd cared enough. Or perhaps I cared too much, about all the little people I'd have had to step on, to get there. To tell the truth, which I try very hard not to do in public, I never was all that ambi-tious. And I was never what you'd call a joiner. So I went my own way, watched my own back, and tried to live by my own definition of honour. That I screwed up so badly wasn't all my fault. I saw my-self as a knight-errant . . . but the damsel in distress stabbed me in the back, my sword shattered on the dragon's hide, and my grail turned out to be the bot-tom of a whiskey bottle. I was going back, to old faces and old haunts and old hurts; and all I could do was hope it would be worth it.

There was no point in hoping not to be noticed. John Taylor is a name to conjure with, in the Night-side. Five years' exile wouldn't have changed that. Not that any of them ever knew the real me, of course. Ask about me in a dozen different places, and you'd get a dozen different answers. I've been called a warlock and a magus, a con man and a trickster, and an honest rogue. They're all wrong, of course. I'd never let anyone get that close. I've been a hero to some, a villain to others, and pretty much everything in between. I can do a few things, beside finding people, some of them quite impressive. When I ask a question, people usually answer. I used to be a dangerous man, even for the Nightside; but that was five years ago. Before the fates broke me, on the wheel of love. I didn't know if I still had it in me to be really dangerous, but I thought so. It's like knocking someone off a bike with a baseball bat; you never really lose the knack.

I've never carried a gun. I've never felt the need.

My father drank himself to death. He never got over finding out his wife wasn't human. I never knew her at all. People on my street took it in turns to look after me, with varying amounts of reluctance and attention, with the result that I never really felt at home anywhere. I have a lot of questions about myself, and I'm still looking for answers. Which is perhaps why I ended up as a private investigator. There's a certain comfort to be had in finding the answers to other people's problems, if you can't solve your own. I wear a long white trench coat when I'm working. Partly because it's expected of me, partly because it's practical, mostly because it establishes an expected image behind which I can conceal the real me. I like to keep people wrong-footed. And I never let anyone get close, any more. As much for their protection as mine.

I sleep alone, I eat everything that's bad for me, and I take care of my own laundry. When I remember. It's important to me to feel self-sufficient. Not dependent on anyone. I have bad luck with women, but I'd be the first to admit it's mostly my fault. Despite my life I'm still a Romantic, with all the problems that brings. My closest female friend is a bounty hunter, who operates exclusively in the Nightside. She tried to kill me once. I don't bear a grudge. It was just business.

I drink too much, and mostly I don't care. I value its numbing qualities. There's a lot I prefer not to remember.

And now, thanks to Joanna Barrett and her errant daughter, I was heading back into Hell. Back into a place where people have been trying to kill me for as long as I remember, for reasons I've never understood. Back into the only place where I ever feel really alive. I'm more than just another private detective, in the Nightside. It was one of the reasons why I left. I didn't like what I was becoming.

But as I headed down into the Underground system below London's streets, with Joanna Barrett in tow, damn if it didn't feel like coming home.

It didn't matter which station or line I chose. All routes lead to the Nightside. And the whole point of the Underground is that every rail station looks the same. The same tiled walls, the same ugly machines, the overly bright lights and the oversized movie and advertising posters. The dusty vending machines, that only tourists are dumb enough to actually expect to get something out of. The homeless, sitting or lying in their nests of filthy blankets, begging for spare change, or just glad to be away from the elements for a while. And, of course, the endless tramp of hurrying feet. Of shoppers, commuters, tourists, businessmen, and media types, always in a hurry to be somewhere else. London hasn't quite reached saturation point yet, like Tokyo, where they have to employ people to forcibly squeeze the last few travellers into a carriage, so the doors will close; but we're getting there.

Joanna stuck close to me as I led the way through the tunnels. It was clear she didn't care for her surroundings, or the crowds. No doubt she was used to better things, like stretch limousines with a uniformed chauffeur and chilled champagne always at the ready. I tried not to smile as I led her through the crush of the crowds. Turned out she didn't carry change on her, so I ended up having to pay for tickets for both of us. I even had to show her how to work the machines with her ticket.

The escalators were all working for once, and we made our way deeper into the system. I took turnings at random, trusting to my old instincts to guide me, until finally I spotted the sign I was looking for. It was written in a language only those in the know would even recognise, let alone understand. Enochian, in case you're interested. An artificial language, created long ago for mortals to talk with angels, though I only ever met one person who knew how to pronounce it correctly. I grabbed Joanna by the arm and hustled her into the side tunnel underneath the sign. She jerked her arm free angrily, but allowed me to urge her through the door marked *Maintenance*. Her protests stopped abruptly as she found herself in what appeared to be a closet, half-full of scarecrows in British Rail uniforms. Don't ask. I pulled the door shut behind us, and there was a blessed moment of peace as the door separated us from the roar of the crowds. There was a phone on the wall. I picked it up. There was no dialling tone. I spoke a single word into the receiver.

"Nightside."

I put the phone back and looked expectantly at the wall. Joanna looked at me, mystified. And then the dull grey wall split in two, from top to bottom, both sides grinding apart in a steady shuddering movement, to form a long narrow tunnel. The bare walls of the tunnel were bloodred, like an opened wound, and the sourceless light was dim and smoky. It smelled of ancient corrupt perfumes and crushed flowers. A murmur of many voices came from within the tunnel, rising and falling. Snatches of music faded in and out, like so many competing radio signals. Somewhere a cloister bell was ringing, a lost and lonely, doleful sound.

"You expect me to go into *that*?" said Joanna, finding her voice at last. "It looks like the road to Hell!"

"Close," I said calmly. "It's the way to the Nightside. Trust me; this part of the journey is quite safe."

"It feels *bad*," Joanna said quietly, staring fascinated into the tunnel, like a bird at a snake. "It feels . . . unnatural."

"Oh, it's all of that. But it's the best way to get to your daughter. If you can't handle this, turn back now. It's only going to get worse."

Her head came up, and her mouth firmed. "You lead the way."

"Of course."

I stepped forward into the tunnel, and Joanna was right there behind me. And so we left the everyday world behind.

We emerged from the connecting tunnel onto a station platform that at first glance was no different than what you'd expect. Joanna took a deep breath of relief. I didn't say anything. It was better for her to notice things for herself. The wall closed silently behind us as I led Joanna down the platform. It was five years since I'd last been here, but nothing had really changed. The cream-tiled walls were spattered here and there with old dried bloodstains, deep gouges that might have been clawmarks, and all kinds of graffiti. As usual, someone had spelt Cthulhu wrongly.

On the curving wall opposite the platform, the list of destinations hadn't changed. *Shadows Fall. Nightside. Haceldama. Street of the Gods.* The posters were still strange, disturbing, like scenes from dreams best forgotten. Famous faces advertised films and places and services of the kind normally only discussed in whispers. The people crowding the platform were a sight in themselves, and I enjoyed Joanna's reactions. It was clear she would have liked to stop and stare open-mouthed, but she was damned if she'd give me the satisfaction. So she stumbled on, wide eyes darting from one unexpected sight to the next.

Here and there buskers were playing unfamiliar tunes, their caps on the floor before them, holding coins from all kinds of places, some of which no longer existed, and a few that never had. One man sang a thirteenth-century ballad of unrequited love in plain-chant Latin, while not far away another sang Bob Dylan verses backwards, accompanying himself on air guitar. The guitar was slightly out of tune. I dropped a few coins into both their caps. Never know when you might need a little extra credit in the karma department.

Further down the platform, a stooped neanderthal in a smart business suit was talking animatedly with a bored-looking dwarf in full Nazi SS uniform. A noble from Queen Elizabeth I's court, complete with ruff and slashed silks, was chatting amiably with a gorgeous six-foot transvestite in full chorus girl outfit, and it was hard to tell which of them looked more extreme. A woman in futuristic space armour and a nude man covered in tattoos and splashes of woad were eating things on sticks that were still wriggling. Joanna had come to a full stop by now. I tapped her on the shoulder, and she all but jumped out of her skin.

"Try not to be a tourist," I said dryly.

"What . . ." She had to stop and try again. "What is this place? Where have you brought me? And who the hell are these people?"

I shrugged. "This is the quickest way to the Nightside. There are others. Some official, some not. Anyone can walk down the wrong street, open the wrong door, and end up in the Nightside. Most of them don't last long, though. London and the Nightside have rubbed up against each other for so long now that the barriers are getting dangerously thin. Someday they'll all come crashing down, and all the poisons in the Nightside will come spilling out; but I plan to be safely dead and in my grave by then. However, this is still the safest way."

"And these people?"

"Just people, going about their lives. You're seeing a part of the world most of you never get to know about. The underside, the hidden paths, walked by secret people on secret business, pursuing goals and missions we can only guess at. There are more worlds than we know, or would wish to know, and most of them send people through the Nightside sooner or later. You can meet all sorts here, in the Underground, and never know harm as long as the ancient Truce holds. Everyone comes to the Nightside. Myths and legends, travellers and explorers, visitors from higher or lower dimensions. Immortals. Deathwalkers. Psychonauts. Try not to stare."

I led her down the platform, and it was a mark of how shaken she was that she didn't have a single comment to make. She didn't even object to my holding her arm again. Without looking round, without interrupting their conversations or in any way acknowledging my presence, the people ahead of us moved back out of the way to let us pass. A few made the sign of the cross when they thought I wasn't looking, and older warding signs against evil. It seemed I hadn't been forgotten after all. A vicar in a shabby grey cloak, with a pristine white collar and a grey blindfold over his eyes, was hawking his wares before us, a much-travelled suitcase open at his feet.

"Crow's feet!" he yelled, in a harsh, strident voice. "Holy water! Hexes! Wooden stakes and silver bullets! You know you need them! Don't come crying to me if you end up limping home with someone else's spleen instead of your own!"

He broke off as Joanna and I approached. He sniffed the air suspiciously, cocking his great blind head to one side. His fingers worked busily at a rosary made from human fingerbones. He stepped forward suddenly to block our way and stabbed an accusing finger at me.

"John Taylor!" he snapped, almost spitting out the words. "Damnation's child! Demonspawn and Abomination! Bane of all the Chosen! Avaunt! Avaunt!"

"Hello, Pew," I said easily. "Good to bump into you again. Still working the old act, I see. How's business?"

"Oh, not too bad thanks, John." Pew smiled vaguely in my direction, putting aside his official Voice for the moment. "My wares are like travel insurance; no-one ever really believes they'll need it, until it's too late. *It can't happen to me,* they whine. But of course, in the Nightside it can, and it will. Suddenly and violently and usually quite horribly too. I'm saving lives here, if they'd only pay attention, the fools. So; what are you doing back here, John? I thought you had more sense. You know the Nightside isn't good for you."

"I'm working a case. Don't worry; I won't be stopping."

"That's what they all say," growled Pew, shifting his broad shoulders uneasily inside his threadbare cloak. "Still, we all do what we have to, I suppose. Who are you looking for this time?"

"Just a runaway. Teenager called Catherine Barrett. Don't suppose the name means anything to you?"

"No. But then, I'm pretty much out of the loop these days, by my own choice. Hard times are coming . . . word of advice, boy. I hear things, bad things. Something new has come into the Nightside. And people have been mentioning your name again. Watch your back, boy. If anyone's going to kill you, I'd much rather it was me."

He turned away abruptly and took up his piercing cry again. There's no-one closer, more like family, than old enemies.

The platform shook, there was a blast of approaching air, and a train roared into the station and slowed to a stop—a long shining silver bullet of a train, with no windows anywhere. The carriages were solid tubes of steel, with only the heavily reinforced doors standing out against their shimmering perfection. The doors hissed open, and people poured in and out. I was ready to take Joanna by the arm again, but it wasn't necessary. She strode into the carriage before her without hesitating, her head held high. I followed her in and sat down beside her.

The carriage was almost empty, for which I was grateful. I've never liked being crowded. All kinds of things can hide in a crowd. The man sitting opposite

us was reading a Russian newspaper with great concentration. The date below the masthead was from a
week in the future. Further down the immaculately
clean carriage sat a young woman kitted out in full
Punk regalia, right down to the multiple face pierc-
ings and fierce green mohawk rising up from her
shaved head. She was reading an oversized leather-
bound Holy Bible. The pages appeared to be blank,
but the white on white of her unblinking eyes marked
her as a graduate of the Deep School, and I knew that
for her and her alone, the pages were full of awful
wisdom.

Joanna was looking around the carriage, and I
tried to see it through her eyes. The complete lack of
windows made it feel more like a cell than a con-
veyance, and the strong smell of disinfectant reminded me irresistibly of a dentist's surgery. There
was no map anywhere. People who took this train
knew where they were going.

"Why aren't there any windows?" said Joanna,
after a while.

"Because you don't want to see what's outside," I
said. "We have to travel through strange, harsh,
places to reach the Nightside. Dangerous and unnatural places, that would blast the sight from your eyes
and the reason from your mind. Or so I'm told. I've
never felt like peeking."

"What about the driver? Doesn't he have to see
where he's going?"

"I'm not convinced there is a driver," I said thoughtfully. "I don't know anyone who's ever seen one. I think the trains have been running this route for so long now that they're quite capable of running themselves."

"You mean there's no-one human at the controls?"

"Probably better that way. Humans are so limited." I smiled at her shocked face. "Sorry you came yet?"

"No."

"Don't worry. You will be."

And that was when something from outside crashed against the side of the carriage opposite us, throwing the Russian to the floor. He carefully gathered up his paper and went to sit further down. The heavy metal wall dented inwards, slowly yielding under the determined assault from outside. The Punk girl didn't look up from her Bible, though she was silently mouthing the words now. The dents in the metal deepened, and one whole section bowed ominously inwards under unimaginable pressure. Joanna sank back in her seat.

"Take it easy," I said reassuringly. "It can't get in. The train is protected."

She looked at me just a little wildly. Culture shock. I'd seen it before. "Protected?" she said finally.

"Old pacts, agreements; trust me, you really don't

want to know the details. Especially if you've eaten recently."

Outside the carriage, something roared with thwarted rage. It didn't sound at all human. The sound fell slowly away, retreating down the length of the carriage as the train left it behind. The metal wall unhurriedly resumed its original shape, the dents disappearing one by one. And then something, or a series of somethings, ran along the side of the carriage and up onto the roof. Light, hasty, pitterpattering fast, moving in unison, like so many huge insects. The carriage lights flickered briefly. It sounded like there was a whole crowd of them up on the roof, scuttling back and forth. Voices came floating down to us, shrill and high and mixed together, like the same voice speaking in harmony with itself. There was a faint metallic buzz in the elongated vowel sounds that sent a shiver down my spine. The Brittle Sisters of the Hive were on the prowl again.

"Come out, come out, whatever you are," said the chorus of a single voice. "Come out, and play with us. Or let us in, let us in, and we will play with you till you can't stand it anymore. We want to stir our sticky fingers in your gene pool, and sculpt your wombs with our living scalpels . . ."

"Make them shut up," Joanna said tightly. "I can't stand their voices. It's like they're scratching at my brain, trying to get in."

I looked at the Russian and the Punk, but they

were resolutely minding their own business. I looked up at the roof of the carriage.

"Go away and stop bothering us," I said firmly. "There is nothing for you here, by terms of Treaty and sacrifice."

"Who dares address us so?" said the many voices in one, almost drowned out by the constant clattering of their taloned feet on the steel roof.

"This is John Taylor," I said clearly. "Don't make me have to come up there."

There was a long pause. They were all very still, until eventually the inhuman chorus said "Then farewell, sweet prince, and do not forget us when you come into your kingdom."

A scurrying of insect feet and they were all gone, and the train rocked on its way in silence. The Russian and the Punk looked at me, and then looked quickly away before I could meet their gaze. Joanna was looking at me too. Her gaze was steady, but her voice couldn't quite manage it.

"They knew you. What did they mean?"

"I don't know," I said. "I've never known. That's always been my problem. There are a great many mysteries in the Nightside, and much against my will, I'm one of them."

No-one else had anything to say, all the way to the Nightside.

THREE

Neon Noir

We came up out of the Underground like souls emerging from the underworld, with chattering throngs of people surging endlessly past in both directions. The train was already long gone, hurrying off as though glad to be leaving. The slow-moving escalators were packed with new travellers and supplicants, all carefully not looking at each other. No-one wanted to draw attention to themselves until they'd got their bearings. The few cold-eyed souls who looked openly about them were the predators and chickenhawks, picking out their prey for later. No-one looked openly at me, but there were a hell of a lot of sidelong glances, and not a few whispers. So much for a quiet visit. The only thing that moves faster than the speed of light is gossip in the Nightside.

Still, the crowd was much as I remembered. Boys, girls, and a few others, all looking for a good time. Business as usual on the dark side of the city. Up on the street, they spilled out of the train station, sniffing freedom and opportunities on the crisp air, and scattered into the endless night, hot on the trail of their own salvations and damnations. Joanna stumbled to a halt inside a dozen paces; wide-eyed, shell-shocked, transfixed by the wonders and strangeness of a whole new world.

This vibrant new city was almost overpoweringly alive; all fever-bright colours and jet-black shadows, welcoming and embracing, frightening and intimidating, seductive and hateful, all at once. Bright neon gleamed everywhere, sharp and gaudy, shiny as shop-soiled tinsel; an endless come-on to suckers and victims and all the lonely souls. Enticing signs beckoned the unwary into all kinds of clubs, promising dark delights and unfamiliar pleasures, drinking and dancing with strangers in smoke-filled rooms, the thrill that never ends, life in the fast lane with no crash barriers anywhere. Sex licked its lips and cocked a hip. It was all dangerous as Hell and twice as much fun.

Damn, it was good to be back.

People surged up and down the street, in all their

many variations, from the unnatural to the unlikely, all of them intent on their own pursuits, while the roar of traffic never stopped. Every vehicle moved at great speed, stopping for nothing, in stark and noisy contrast to the packed city streets of everyday London, where the general speed of traffic hasn't changed much in centuries; thanks to the appalling congestion it still averages out at around ten miles an hour. No matter how important you think you are. Though at least these days the streets stink of petrol fumes rather than horse shit.

You can't step in petrol fumes.

Many of the sleek and gleaming vehicles darting through the Nightside had to be new to Joanna; shapes and sizes and even concepts that had never known the light of day; some of them powered from sources best not thought about too much, if you wanted to sleep at night. Taxis that ran on debased holy water, limousines that ran on fresh blood, ambulances that ran on distilled suffering. You can turn a profit from anything, in the Nightside. I had to take Joanna by the arm as she drifted unrealisingly too close to the edge of the pavement.

"Careful!" I said loudly in her ear. "Some of those things aren't really cars. And some of them are hungry."

But she wasn't listening to me. She'd looked up at the sky, and her upturned face was full of wonder and awe. I smiled, and looked up too. Deep deep black, the sky, falling away forever, blazing with the light of thousands and thousands of stars, far more than you'd ever seen above any earthly city, dominated by a full moon a dozen times larger than the poor pallid thing Joanna was used to seeing. I've never been sure whether the moon really is bigger in the Nightside, or whether it's just *closer.* Maybe someday someone with serious money will hire me to find out.

I looked back at Joanna, but she was still clearly struggling to find her equilibrium, so I just stood there and looked mildly about me. It had been five years, after all. But it all seemed much as I remembered it. The same quietly desperate people, hurrying down the same rain-slicked streets, heading eagerly into the same old honey traps. Or perhaps I was just being cynical. There were wonders and marvels to be found in the Nightside, sights and glories to be savoured and clutched to your heart forever; you just had to look that little bit harder to find them, that was all. The Nightside is really just like any other major city, only amplified, intensified, like the city streets we walk in dreams and nightmares.

There was a kiosk beside the station entrance selling racks of shrink-wrapped T-shirts. I studied some of the legends on the shirtfronts. *Good boys go to Heaven, bad boys go to the Nightside. My mother took thalidomine, and all I got was this lousy hammer toe.* And the perennial *Michael Jackson died for our sins.* I snorted quietly. The usual tourist stuff.

Joanna turned suddenly to look at me, her mouth snapping shut as though she'd only just realised it was hanging open.

"Welcome to the Nightside," I said, smiling. "Abandon all taste, ye who enter here."

"It's night," she said numbly. "What happened to the rest of the day? It was only just starting to get dark when we left."

"I told you; it's always night here. People come here for the things they can't find anywhere else; and a lot of those things can only thrive in the dark."

She shook her head slowly. "We're really not in Kansas any more, are we? Guess I'll just have to try and keep an open mind."

"Oh, I wouldn't do that," I said solemnly. "You never know what might walk in."

She gave me a hard look. "I can never tell when you're joking."

"Neither can I sometimes, in the Nightside. It's that kind of place. Life, death and reality are all flexible concepts here."

A street gang came whooping and hollering down the street towards us, shouldering people out of their way, and playfully pushing some out into the road to dodge the traffic, which didn't even bother with horns, let alone slowing down. The gang members laughed and elbowed each other and drank heavily from bottles they passed back and forth between them. They were loud and obnoxious and loving every minute of it, and the threat of sudden violence hung about them like bad body odour. There were thirteen of them, wearing polished leathers and hanging chains, with bright tribal colours on their faces. Their teeth came to sharp points, and they wore strap-on devil's horns on their foreheads. They came roaring and swaggering down the street, swearing nastily at anyone who didn't get out of their way fast enough and looking eagerly round for some trouble to get into. Preferably the kind where someone got hurt.

And then one of them spotted Joanna, recognising her immediately as a newcomer. Easy target, money on the hoof, and a woman as well. He clued in his brothers, and they surged forward, moving with a purpose. I stepped forward, out of the shadows, and put myself between them and Joanna. The gang lurched to a sudden halt, and I could hear my name on their lips. Their hands were quickly full of knives, long slender blades gleaming sullenly in the neon light. I smiled at the gang, and some of them started backing away. I let my smile widen, and the gang turned abruptly and walked away. Mostly, I felt relieved. I hadn't been sure whether I was bluffing or not.

"Thank you," said Joanna, her voice quite steady. "I was concerned there, for a moment. Who were they?"

"Demons."

"Is that the name of their gang?"

"No, they're demons, playing at being a street gang. Probably out on day release. We get all sorts here."

She thought about that. "They were frightened of you."

"Yes."

"What makes you so special, here?"

I had to smile. "Damned if I know. Let's just say I have something of a reputation in the Nightside. Or at least, I used to. Be interesting to see how much currency my name still has here, in some of the places we're going to have to visit."

Joanna looked around her. "Shouldn't we alert the police, or something? Those . . . demons might attack someone else."

"There are no police operating in the Nightside," I explained patiently.

"Not many laws, either. Anything goes here; that's part of the attraction. There are . . . Authorities. Those with power to punish serious transgressors. Pray we don't run into them."

Joanna took a deep breath, and let it out slowly. "All right; I can handle this. I came here to find my daughter, and I can cope with anything if it helps me retrieve her. You said you had a gift for finding people. Show me."

"It's not that simple."

"Why did I just know you were going to say that?"

I met her accusing gaze steadily, choosing my words with more than usual care. "I have a gift. Call it magic, or esp, or whatever current buzzword you feel most comfortable with. I can use that gift to track down missing people or objects, things that are hidden from normal view and normal investigative procedures. It only works here in the Nightside, where the laws of reality aren't as strictly nailed down as they might be. But I have to be very careful how and where and when I use it. I have enemies here. Bad people. Using my gift is like shining a bright light in a dark place. It attracts attention. My enemies can follow the light to find me. And kill me."

"Who are these enemies?" said Joanna, and for the first time there was something like concern in her cool blue eyes. "Why are they so keen to kill you? What did you do? And why is a man who can scare off demons so frightened by these people?"

"They are many, and I am one. They've been after me for as long as I can remember. It started when I was still a child. They once burned down a whole city block, trying to get to me. Over the years they've killed a lot of people who were close to me. It's a wonder I have any friends left. They aren't always out there . . . sometimes I think they're afraid of me. Either way, I've never been able to find out who they are, or why they want me dead so badly. I'm safe in the mundane world. They can't track me there. But this is their territory as well as mine. I only agreed to take on this case because it seemed so simple and straightforward. With just a little bit of luck, we should be able to track down your daughter, put the two of you together for a little heart-to-heart, and then get the hell out of here. Without anyone who matters knowing I'm here. Now hush, and let me concentrate. The briefer I can keep this, the better."

I concentrated, reaching deep down inside myself, and my gift unfolded like a flower, blossoming up to fill my mind, then spilling out onto the night. My third eye opened wide, my private eye, and suddenly I could See. And there she was, right before me; Cathy Barrett's after-image, glowing and shimmering on the night. The ghost she left behind, stamped on Time by her presence; a semi-transparent wraith drawn in pastel shades. Passing pedestrians walked around and through her without seeing her. I concentrated on her image, rewinding the past, watching closely as Cathy emerged again from the Underground station entrance and looked around her, dazed and delighted at the new world she'd found. She was wearing Salvation Army cast-offs, but she looked happy and healthy enough. Cathy looked around suddenly, as though someone had called her name. She smiled then, a wide happy smile that transformed her face. She looked radiant, delighted, as though she'd found an old dear friend in an unexpected place. She started off down the street, hurrying towards . . . something. Something I couldn't See or sense, but it pulled her to it with a single-minded, implacable purpose, like a moth drawn to a blow-torch.

I replayed the image from the beginning, watching again as the ghost from the past came tripping out of the station entrance. Cathy's imprint was still too clear and uncorrupted to be more than a few weeks old at most. The impressions I was getting from the image puzzled me. Unlike most runaways Cathy hadn't come into the Nightside looking to hide from someone, or forget some past pain. She'd come here with a purpose, looking for some specific thing or person. Something or someone here had *called* her. I frowned, and opened up my mind just a crack further, but there was nothing unusual beating on the night air, no siren call strong enough to summon people from the safety of the mundane world.

Unless the caller was shielded from me. Which was a worrying thought. There's not much that can hide from me, when I put my mind to it. I'm John Taylor, damn it. I find things. Whether they want to be found or not.

Unless . . . I was dealing with one of the Major Powers.

I braced myself and pushed my mind all the way open. The hidden world snapped into focus all around me. Old paths of power criss-crossed each other, cutting unnoticed through the material world, burning so brightly I had to look away. Ghosts stamped and howled, going through their endless paces over and over, trapped in moments of Time like insects caught in amber. Wispy insubstantial giants strode slowly through the city, not deigning to look down on all the tiny mortals beneath them. The Faerie and the Transient Beings and the Awful Folk went about their various mysterious businesses, and none of them so much as looked at me. And still there was no trace anywhere of whatever had called so beguilingly to Cathy Barrett.

I shut my mind down again, layer by careful layer, re-establishing my shields. It had been so long since I'd had a chance to glory in the Sights of my gift that I'd forgotten all about being cautious. For a time there, I must have shone like the sun. Time to get this show on the road. I reached out and took Joanna firmly by the hand, linking her mind to mine, and she gasped as she saw the street through my private eye. She saw Cathy's translucent image, and called out to her, starting forward. Immediately I let go of her hand, and shut everything down, tamping down the edges of my gift with great thoroughness, so that not even a spark of light could get out to betray me. Joanna rounded on me angrily.

"What happened? Where is she? I saw her!"

"You saw an image from the past," I said carefully. "A footprint, left in Time. Cathy hasn't been here for at least two weeks, more than enough time for her to get into some serious trouble. But at least now we know for sure that she did get here, and that she was alive and well two weeks ago. Did you see the look on her face? She came here for a reason. She was headed somewhere specific."

Joanna's face had quickly resumed its usual chilly mask, as though she was ashamed I'd caught her showing actual emotions. When she spoke, her voice was entirely calm again. "Specific. Is that good or bad?"

"Depends," I said honestly. "This is the Nightside. She could be anywhere by now. She might have found friends, protection, enlightenment, or damnation. They're all pretty cheap here. I think . . . I'm going to need a little help on this one. How would you like to visit the oldest established bar and night-club in the world?"

One side of her dark red mouth twitched in something that might have been a smile. "Sounds good to me. I could use a stiff drink. Hell, I could use several stiff drinks and an adrenaline chaser. What's the name of this place?"

I grinned. "Strangefellows."

FOUR

Everyone Goes to Strangefellows.
If They Know What's Good For Them.

You get to Strangefellows, the oldest drinking hole, conversation pit and scumbag attractor in the history of Mankind, by walking down the kind of streets that raise the hairs on the back of your neck, and then slipping into a side alley that isn't always there. Mostly, I think it's ashamed to be associated with such a dive. The alley is dimly lit and the street had cobbles. The entrance to Strangefellows is a flat slab of steel set flush with the grimy wall. Above the door is a small but dignified neon sign that spells out the name of the bar in ancient Sanskrit. The owner doesn't believe in advertising. He doesn't need to. If you're meant to find your way to the oldest pub in England, you will. And if you're not, you could search all the days of your life and never find it. There's no waiting list to get in, but the dues can be murder. Sometimes literally. I translated the sign for Joanna, and she looked at it expressionlessly.

"Is this a gay bar?"

I had to smile. "No. Just a place where the stranger people in the world can come to drink in peace and quiet. No-one bothers you, no-one will expect you to talk sports, politics or religion, and no-one will ask for your autograph. Good and Bad can buy each other drinks, and neutrality is strictly enforced. Strangefellows has been around, in various identities, for centuries. No-one's really sure how old it is, but it's always been a bar of some kind. The last time I was here, the current incarnation was decidedly upmarket. Glamorous in a threatening kind of way, with excellent booze and an . . . interesting clientele. But identities can change fast in the Nightside, so once we get in there stick close to me, hang on to your bag and don't talk to any strange women."

"I have been to nightclubs before," Joanna said frostily.

"Not like this one, you haven't."

I walked up to the door, and it swung slowly open before me. Though I hated to admit it, I was more than a little relieved. The door only opens to people in good standing with the owner, and I hadn't been sure just what my standing was, after so long away. We hadn't exactly parted on good terms. Hell, I still had money owing on my bar bill. But the door had opened, so I made a point of walking in like I owned the place, with Joanna looking at her most alluring and intimidating at my side. Keep your chin up, and your gaze steady. Remember, they can smell fear here.

I stopped in the middle of the foyer, and looked about me, taking my time. The old place hadn't changed much after all. The same Tudor furniture, with people draped over them like bendy toys, trying to sleep some of it off before they had to go home. The same obscene murals on the walls and ceilings, some of them in bas-relief. The same stains on the Persian carpet. I felt positively nostalgic. I glanced at Joanna, but she was carefully maintaining the straightest of straight faces. I led the way forward, stepping over outstretched legs where necessary, until we could look down the metal stairs and into the wide stone-walled pit that held the bar proper.

The first word that came to mind on seeing the bar again was *seedy*. Though *sleazy* came a very close second. Clearly the upmarket experiment hadn't taken. I led the way down the stairs, which clanged noisily under our feet, by design. The bar's patrons preferred not to be taken by surprise. There was the usual sea of mismatched tables and chairs, with booths at the far end for those who felt in need of a little extra privacy. Or somewhere to hide a body for a while. The lights were always kept low—partly for atmosphere, and partly so you couldn't get too good a look at your surroundings. Or your fellow company. Most of the tables were occupied, by the kind of mixed crowd that reminded me why I'd left the Nightside in the first place. I recognised a lot of the faces; though most of them were ostentatiously not looking at me. The usual babble of raised voices was half–drowned out by loud heavy metal rock being blasted through concealed speakers. The close unmoving air was heavy with smoke, some of it legal, some of it earthly. A sign on the wall at the bottom of the stairs said *Enter At Your Own Risk.* Joanna drew my attention to it.

"Are they serious?"

"Sure," I said calmly. "The bar food's terrible."

"So is the ambience," Joanna said dryly. "I can feel my credit rating dropping just from being here. Tell me we're here for a purpose."

"We're looking for information," I said patiently. It never hurts to spell it out for clients, especially when you know it irritates them. "We need to know who or what summoned Cathy into the Nightside, and where she went after my gift lost her. You can find the answer to practically any question at Strangefellows, if you know the right people to ask."

"And if you know the right palms to grease?"

"You see; you're learning. Money doesn't just talk

in the Nightside; it shouts and screams and twists arms. It helps that most of the real movers and shakers have passed through here at one time or another, on their way up or on their way down. There are those who say this place has been around since civilisation began."

Joanna sniffed. "Doesn't look like it's been cleaned much since then, either."

"Merlin Satanspawn was buried here, under the wine cellar, after the fall of Logres. He still makes the occasional appearance, to keep everyone honest. Being dead doesn't stop you from being a major player, in the Nightside."

"Hold everything. *The* Merlin?"

"I'd hate to think there was more than one. I only saw him manifest once, but it scared the crap out of me."

Joanna shook her head. "I need a very large drink, right now."

"Lot of people feel that way in the Nightside."

I headed for the extended mahogany bar at the end of the room. It was good to be back. I could feel long-buried parts of me waking up and flexing their muscles. Sometimes I hated the Nightside, and sometimes I loved it, but running away to the real world had only served to show me how much I needed it. For all its threats and dangers, its casual brutality and deep-seated wickedness, it was only here that I felt truly alive. And I'd had some good times in this bar, back in my younger days. Admittedly mostly because back then I'd been strictly small change, and no-one gave a damn about who I was, or might be. I led Joanna through the packed tables, and the noise of conversation didn't even slip as we passed. The record on the speakers changed, and the Stranglers began shouting about there being "No More Heroes." The bar's owner's way of letting me know he'd noticed my arrival. Joanna winced at the noise, and put her mouth next to my ear.

"Is this racket all they play here?"

"Pretty much," I said loudly. "This is Alex Morrisey's place, and he plays what he wants. He likes heavy rock, he doesn't believe in being cheerful, and he doesn't take requests. Someone came in here once and asked for Country and Western, and Alex shot him. A lot of people applauded."

We came to the bar. Alex Morrisey was there, as always, a long streak of misery in basic black. He was the latest in a long line of bartender/owners, from a family that had been around longer than it was comfortable to contemplate. It's not clear whether they stick around to protect Merlin, or possibly vice versa, and no-one likes to ask because if you do Alex throws things. It's no secret he'd leave Strangefellows in a moment if he could, but he can't. His family is bound to the bar, by ancient and unpleasant pacts, and Alex can't leave until he can find someone else from his family line to take his place. And since

Alex Morrisey is reputed to be the very last of his long line, it's just another reason for him to act up cranky and take it out on his customers.

The word is Alex was born in a bad mood, and has only got worse since. Permanently seething, viciously unfair just for the hell of it, and notoriously cavalier when it comes to giving you the right change. Though God protect your soul if you hold back one penny when he calls in your marker. He claims to be the true heir to the British Throne, being a (more or less) direct descendant of Uther Pendragon, on the wrong side of several blankets. He also claims he can see people's auras if he bangs his head against the wall just right. He was currently taking his own sweet time about serving another customer, but he knew I was there. Nothing happened in Alex's bar that he didn't know about, sometimes even before you knew you were going to do it. His party trick is to answer a phone just before it rings.

I leaned on the bar and studied him openly. He looked just as I remembered him, appalling and disturbing, in equal measures. Alex had to be in his late twenties by now, but looked ten years older; thin, pale and moody, and always thoroughly vexed about something. His scowl had etched a permanent notch above his nose, and on the few occasions when he smiled, you knew you were in trouble. He always wore black of some description, topped with designer shades and a snazzy black beret perched on the back of his head, to hide the bald spot that appeared when he was still a teenager. Proof if proof were needed, he always said, that God hated him personally. He shaved when he remembered, which wasn't often, and didn't wash the bar's glasses anywhere near often enough. His spiky black hair stuck out in tufts, because he tugged at it a lot, and his personal hygiene bordered on distressing.

He still had a large glamour calendar behind the bar, showing Elvira Mistress of the Dark, in a series of photographic poses that would probably upset her greatly if she ever found out about them, and the designs on the bar coasters were cheerfully pornographic. On the whole, Alex is very bad with women, most of whom don't live down to his expectations. He was married once, and still won't talk about it. And that . . . is Alex Morrisey for you. Pissed off at the entire world and proud of it, and mixer of the worst martinis in the Nightside.

I suppose we're friends. We both put up with a lot of things from each other that we wouldn't tolerate for a second from anyone else.

He finally gave up pretending I wasn't there and slouched along the bar to glare at me.

"I knew it was going to be a bad day when I woke up to find my rabbit's foot had grown itself a new rabbit," he said resentfully. "If I'd known it was a warning you were coming back into my life, I would have locked all the doors and windows and melted down the keys. What do you want?"

"Good to see you again, Alex. How's business?"

He sniffed, loudly. "Takings have dropped so low you'd need an excavator to find any profits, a poltergeist has moved into my cellar and is haunting my beer barrels, turning the taps on and off, and Pale Michael is claiming that since he is now a zombie and officially dead, with a coroner's certificate to prove it, he doesn't have to pay his not inconsiderable bar bill. And now you're here. It's nights like this that make me dream of bloody insurrection, and planting bombs in public places. What are you doing back here, John? You said you were never coming back, and it was the only sensible thing I ever heard you say."

"The lady at my side is Joanna Barrett. Her daughter's gone missing, in the Nightside. And I've drawn a blank."

Alex looked at me over his sunglasses. "I thought you could find anything?"

"So did I. But my gift could only show me so much before I got locked out. Someone's hiding this runaway. I won't be able to pick up her trail again till I can get a lot closer to her. Which means I need a lead. Is Eddie around?"

"Yes, and I do wish he wasn't. He's at his usual table in the corner, scaring off the reputable trade."

And that was when the three yuppies appeared out

of nowhere to surround me. I turned around unhurriedly as I spotted their reflections in the long mirror behind the bar, and looked them over curiously. They seemed fairly generic; all young, all dressed in the very best-cut suits, with razor-trimmed hair, a single ear-ring, and perfectly manicured hands. Old school ties, of course. They all looked very unhappy with me, but the one glaring right into my face seemed vaguely familiar. Joanna, I noticed, was making a point of being distinctly unimpressed with them. Good for her. I leaned back against the bar, and raised a single eyebrow with just the right amount of insolence. The big bad businessman before me pushed his face even closer to mine and breathed spearmint into my face. I hate spearmint.

"John Taylor!" the yuppie said loudly, trying his very best to sound fierce and hard and menacing, in a high-pitched voice that really wasn't suited to it. "John *bloody* Taylor! Oh, God is good, isn't he? Sending you back to me. I always knew you'd come crawling back here someday, Taylor, so I could personally ensure you got what was coming to you!"

"I get the impression you know me," I said calmly. "Can't say the same, I'm afraid. Do I owe you money, by any chance?"

"Don't you dare pretend you don't remember! I told you never to come back here, Taylor. I told you never to show your face here again. You made me look bad."

"It wasn't difficult," observed Alex from behind the bar. He was watching interestedly and making absolutely no move to intervene.

The yuppie pretended he hadn't heard that. Mad as he was, he wasn't stupid enough to upset Alex. He turned the full force of his glare on me, his slightly bulging eyes all but protruding from their sockets, while his two friends did their best to lurk dangerously in the background, being supportive.

"I said I'd do for you, Taylor, if I ever saw you again. Interfering little turd, meddling in the affairs of your betters!"

"Ah," I said, the light finally dawning. "Sorry, but it has been five years. I remember you now. The limited vocabulary and repetitive threats finally rang a bell. Ffinch-Thomas, isn't it? You were in here one night slapping your girl about, because you were in a bad mood. And because you could. I wasn't going to interfere. Really, I wasn't. If she was stupid enough to go about with a hyphenated thug like you, just because you always had the money for the very best booze and blow and clubs, that was her affair. But then you knocked her down, and kicked her in the side till her ribs broke. Giggling while you did it. So I beat the crap out of you, stole all your credit cards, and finished up by throwing you through a window that happened to be closed at the time. As I recall, you made these famous threats of yours while hobbling away at speed, trying to pull bits of glass out of your arse. Anyone else would have derived a useful moral lesson from these events. Alex, I'm surprised you let this little swine back in here."

Alex shrugged, leaning his elbows on the bar. "What can I tell you? His father's something big in the city. Both of them."

The music in the bar broke off suddenly, and the general babble of voices quickly died away as people realised what was happening. There was interest from all sides now, and not a little money changing hands. Everyone wanted to see if John Taylor still had it. I was kind of curious myself.

"You can't talk to me like that," said Ffinch-Thomas, his voice so strained it was practically breaking.

"Of course I can. I just did. Weren't you paying attention?"

He drew a slender golden scythe from inside his jacket, a nasty little instrument expertly crafted to fit his hand. The blade gleamed brightly, and I just knew the edges would be razor-sharp. The other two yuppies drew similar weapons. Must be the latest thing. Druid chic.

"We're going to do it to you," said Ffinch-Thomas, grinning widely. His voice was light and breathy, and his eyes were bright with excitement. "We're going to do it and do it and do it. Make you scream, Taylor. Spread your blood and skin all over the bar, until you beg to be allowed to die. I never believed those stories about you. You just caught me by surprise last time. And after we've made you cry and squeal, we'll stop for a while, so you can watch us do it to your woman. And we'll . . . we'll . . ."

His voice trailed away to nothing as I locked on to his eyes with mine. I'd heard enough. More than enough. Some insects just beg to be stepped on. He stood very still, trying to look away, but he couldn't. I had him. Beads of sweat popped out all over his suddenly grey face, as he tried to turn and run and found he couldn't. He whimpered, and wet himself, a large dark stain spreading across the front of his very expensive trousers. His hand opened, against his will, and the golden scythe tumbled from his nerveless fingers, clattering loudly on the floor in the hushed quiet. He was scared now, really scared. I smiled at him, and blood ran down his cheeks from his staring eyes. He was whining, a thin, trapped, animal sound, and then his eyes rolled up in his head, and he collapsed unconscious on the floor. His two yuppie friends stood gaping down at him, and then they looked at me. They held up their golden scythes with shaking hands, nerving themselves to attack, and Alex raised his voice.

"Lucy! Betty! *Trouble!*"

Lucy and Betty Coltrane were suddenly right there, behind the yuppies. The Coltranes have been Alex's bouncers for years. Tall and formidable bodybuilders, the girls never wore anything more than T-shirt and shorts, the better to show off their impressive muscles. One is blonde and one is brunette, but otherwise there's not much to choose between them. They have a somewhat threatening glamour, and crack nuts by coughing loudly. They fell on the two yuppies, slapped the scythes out of their hands, slammed them back against the bar, kneed them briskly in the privates, and then frog-marched them out. The watching crowd cheered and applauded. A few wolf-whistled. I looked reproachfully at Alex.

"I could have handled them."

He sniffed loudly. "I've seen what happens when you handle things, and it takes ages to mop up the blood afterwards. Here; have one on the house, and for God's sake leave the rest of my customers alone."

I accepted the offered brandy with good grace. It was the nearest Alex could come to an apology. The Coltranes came back and carried off the still-twitching Ffinch-Thomas.

"He'll tell his daddy on you," observed Alex. "And Daddy will not be pleased. He might even be just a bit peeved with you."

"Tell him to take a number," I said, because you have to say things like that in public. God knows I've got enough enemies without making more, but the young Ffinch-Thomas and his type deserve a good slapping now and again. Just on general principles. Joanna had been watching the Coltranes.

"Who . . . *what* are they?"

"My pride and glory," Alex said fondly. "Betty and Lucy Coltrane. Best damned bouncers in the business. Though of course I'd never tell them that. Fiercer than pit bulls and cheaper to run. Married to each other. They had a dog once, but they ate it."

Joanna was looking just a little dazed. "I think we need to go talk with Eddie," I said kindly. "Talk to you later, Alex."

"If you must. I'd bar you, if I thought you'd listen. You're trouble, John, and you always will be."

Heavy rock started up again, loud and driving, and all the various conversations resumed, having decided regretfully that the show was over. Still, they had plenty to talk about now. John Taylor was definitely back, and as sharp as ever. I couldn't have planned it better. A good dramatic scene helps to keep the flies off. Though it can also attract the wrong kind of attention. I headed for the far corner of the pit, Joanna at my side. She was looking at me just a little oddly.

"Don't mind Alex," I said calmly. "He's the only man I know who suffers from permanent PMT."

"Did those women really eat their own dog?"

I shrugged. "Times were hard."

"And just what did you do to that poor bastard?"

"I stared him down."

Joanna gave me a hard look, and then clearly decided not to pursue that any further. Wise of her.

"Who's this Eddie we're going to see? And how can he help us find my daughter?"

"Razor Eddie," I said. "Punk God of the Straight Razor. Supposedly. Got his name quite a few years back, in a street war over territory between neighbouring gangs. Eddie was just fourteen at the time, and already a slick and vicious killer. Expert with a pearl-handled razor, and nasty with it. Already more than a little crazy. In the years that followed, he'd kill for anyone who had the price, or just for a little attention."

"You know the most charming people," murmured Joanna. "How is someone like that going to help us?"

"Wait. It gets better. Eddie went missing. Something happened to him on the Street of the Gods, something he still won't talk about, and when he came back it was as something both more and less than human. Now he sleeps in doorways, lives on handouts and eats leftovers, and wanders where he will, living a life of violent penance for his earlier sins. His chosen victims tend to be the bad guys no-one else can touch. The ones who think they're protected from the consequences of their actions by money or power. They tend to end up being found dead in mysterious, upsetting ways. And that's Razor Eddie; an extremely disturbing agent for the good. The good didn't get a say in the matter."

"You're lecturing me again." For the first time since I'd led her into the Nightside, Joanna looked a little unsettled. "All that matters . . . is whether he can help me find my Cathy. Will he want paying?"

"No. Eddie doesn't have any use for money, any more. But he does still owe me a favour."

"I'd hate to think what for."

"Best not to," I agreed.

We finally came to a halt before a table in a particularly dark and shadowy corner of the stone-walled pit. And behind that table, Razor Eddie, a painfully thin presence in an oversized grey coat apparently held together by accumulated filth and grease. Just looking at it was enough to make you itch, and the smell was appalling. Rats have been known to jump back into open sewers, just to get away from the smell of an approaching Razor Eddie. He hadn't changed at all in five years. The same hollowed face and fever-bright eyes, the same disturbing presence. Being around Eddie was as close as most people get to death before the real thing comes looking for them. He likes to drink at Strangefellows, somewhere at the back, away from bright lights. No-one judges him, and no-one bothers him. His drinks are on the house, and in return Eddie never kills anyone actually on the premises.

He had a bottle of designer water on the table in front of him, with flies crawling all over it. More flies buzzed around Eddie, except for the ones that got too close, and fell dead out of the air. I smiled at Eddie, and he nodded gravely back. I pulled up a chair opposite him. The smell was every bit as bad as I'd remembered it, but I like to think it didn't show in my face. Joanna pulled up a chair beside me, trying hard to breathe only through her mouth. When Eddie spoke, his voice was low, controlled, almost ghostly.

"Hello, John. Welcome home. You're looking well. Why is it you only ever come to see me when you want something?"

"You're not always the easiest man to find, Eddie. And, you're a spooky bastard. So, how are things? Killed anyone interesting recently?"

The ghost of a smile moved across his pale lips. "No-one you'd know. I hear you're looking for a runaway."

Joanna started. "How did you know that?"

"Word gets around, in the Nightside," said Eddie. He turned his disturbingly bright eyes on me. "Try the Fortress."

I nodded. I should have thought of that one myself. "Thanks, Eddie."

"You'll find Suzie there."

"Oh good," I said, trying to sound pleased. Suzie and I have a history. I was about to push back my chair when Eddie turned suddenly to look at Joanna, who started again under the impact of his gaze.

"You be careful around this man, miss. John isn't the safest of people to keep company with."

"Anything specific in mind, Eddie?" I said carefully.

"There are people looking for you, John."

"There are always people looking for me."

Eddie smiled gently. "These are *bad* people."

I waited, but he had nothing more to say. I nodded my thanks and rose to my feet. Joanna scrambled quickly to hers. I took her back to the bar. She breathed deeply all the way, and then shuddered suddenly.

"*Awful* little man. And what was that stench? I swear, he smelled like something that had died and then been dug up again."

"There are things about Razor Eddie it's best not to ask," I said wisely. "For our own peace of mind."

We were back at the bar again. Alex glowered at me in greeting. I looked at Joanna.

"You wait here, while I get word to the Fortress that we're coming. It's best not to surprise people with that many guns."

I moved off down the bar to use the courtesy phone. But even as I hit the numbers, listened to a recorded voice from the Fortress and left a brief message, I was still listening carefully to Joanna as she talked with Alex. Keep a close eye on your enemies, but a closer one on your friends. And clients. You tend to live longer that way, in my business. Alex gave Joanna what he thinks is his ingratiating smile. She didn't smile back.

"I'll have a large whiskey. Single malt. No ice."

"At last," said Alex. "A civilised drinker. You wouldn't believe what I get asked for some nights.

Designer beers and flavoured spirits and bloody cocktails with soft porn names. One guy actually wanted a piledriver, vodka with prune juice. Animal."

He poured Joanna a generous measure in a reasonably clean glass. She looked at him thoughtfully. "You know John Taylor."

"For my sins, yes."

"How well do you know him?"

"As well as he'll let me," said Alex, unusually serious. He has a weakness for blondes, especially ones that don't take any shit from him. That's why I left them alone together. Alex leaned across the bar to Joanna. "John doesn't believe in letting people in. And it has been five years . . . Still, I knew he'd be back someday. This place has its claws in him. Born in the Nightside, he'll die in the Nightside, and it won't be of old age. Always has to be the white knight, riding in to rescue some poor bastard caught between a rock and a hard place. The ones with no-one else to turn to. John's always been a sucker for a hard luck story, and it would appear he's still arrogant enough to believe he knows what's best for everyone."

"Why did he become a private detective?"

"He has a gift for finding things. Only decent thing he got from his parents. You know the story? Everyone here does. How John's father killed himself by inches after finding out the woman he married wasn't . . . entirely human. I feel much the same about my ex-wife. May she rest in peace."

"I'm sorry," said Joanna. "When did she die?"

"She didn't," said Alex. "It's just wishful thinking on my part."

"Can I trust Taylor?" said Joanna forcefully.

"You can trust him to do what he feels is best. Which may or may not be what you want. So watch yourself."

"Razor Eddie said we should go to the Fortress."

Alex winced at the name, but nodded. "Sounds about right."

"What is it? Another bar?"

"Hardly. The Fortress is a heavily fortified refuge for people who've been abducted by aliens. A whole lot of them got together, bought a whole lot of guns, and made it clear to all and sundry that they weren't being taken again without one hell of a fight. There's a television camera in every room, so they can be watched over even while they sleep. Some of them even have explosive devices taped to their bodies, ready to be triggered at a moment's notice. Word is there's enough ammo and bombs in that place to fight a fairly major war."

"Does it work?" said Joanna.

Alex shrugged. "They're not the kind of people you ask personal questions of. They're always on the lookout for Men in Black. Anyway, over the years the Fortress has become something of a haven for anyone who needs help or protection, or just somewhere safe and secure to crash for a few days. A lot of runaways pass through the Fortress."

"Are they good people?"

"Oh sure. Paranoid, violent and crazy as a cat on crack, but . . ."

I decided I'd heard enough. I put the phone down and went back to join them. Alex might or might not have known I was listening. It didn't matter. I nodded to Joanna.

"All I can get is the answerphone. We'll have to go round there and ask in person."

"Can't wait," said Joanna. She downed the last of her drink in one. Alex blinked respectfully a few times. Joanna slammed the glass down on the bar. "Put it on Taylor's tab."

"You're learning," said Alex.

I headed for the metal stairs, Joanna at my side. No-one looked around as we passed. Joanna looked at me suddenly.

"John?"

"Yes?"

"Did they *really* eat their dog?"

FIVE

The Harrowing

We left Strangefellows, stepping out into the sullen gloom of the back alley, and the solid steel door shut itself firmly behind us. On the whole, things hadn't gone too badly. Eddie had come up with a solid lead, no-one serious had tried to kill me, and Alex hadn't even mentioned my long-standing bar bill. Presumably because he knew a rich client when he saw one. I'd hate to think he was getting soft. Joanna looked vaguely about her, frowned, and hugged herself tightly, shivering suddenly. Understandable. The alley was freezing cold, with thick whorls of hoar-frost on the walls and cobbled ground. The night had turned distinctly wintry in the short time we'd been inside. Joanna looked at me accusingly, her breath steaming thickly on the still air.

"All right, what happened to the weather? It was a nice balmy summer night when we went through that door."

"We don't really have weather, as such, in the Nightside," I explained patiently. "Or seasons, either. Here, the night never ends. Think of temperature changes here less as weather, and more as moods. Just the city, expressing itself. If you don't like the current conditions, wait a minute, and something new but equally distressing will come along. Sometimes, I think we get the weather we deserve here. Which is probably why it rains a lot."

I started off down the alley, and Joanna strode along beside me, her heels clacking loudly on the cobbles. She was working her way up to asking me something intrusive. I could tell.

"Eddie said bad people were looking for you," she said finally.

"Don't worry. The Nightside is a big place to get lost in. We'll have found your daughter and be long gone before anyone can catch up to us."

"If people are always looking for you here . . . why don't you just stay out of the Nightside?"

I did her the courtesy of considering the matter for a few moments. It was a serious question, and deserved a serious answer. "I tried, for five long years. But the Nightside is seductive. There's nothing in everyday London to match it. It's like living in colour, instead of black and white. Everything's more intense here, more primal. Things matter more, here. Beliefs, actions, lives . . . can have more significance, in the great scheme of things. But in the end, it all comes down to the fact that I can make a much better living here, than I can in London. My gift only works in the Nightside. I'm somebody, here, even if 1 don't always like who that person is. Besides, you can't let anyone tell you where you can and can't go. It's bad for business."

"Alex said this was your home. Where you belong."

"Home is where the heart is," I said. "And most people don't dare reveal their heart here. Someone would eat it."

"Eddie said they were *bad* people," Joanna said stubbornly. "And he looked like the kind who would know *bad*. Be honest with me. Are we in any immediate danger?"

"Always, in the Nightside. All kinds of people end up here, drawn and driven by passions and needs that can't properly be expressed or satisfied anywhere else. And a lot of them like to play rough. But most of them know better than to mess with me."

She looked at me, amused. "Hard man."

"Only when I have to be."

"Are you armed?"

"I don't carry a gun," I said. "I've never felt the need."

"I can look after myself too," she said suddenly.

"I don't doubt it," I assured her. "Or I would never have let you come with me."

"So, who's this Suzie, that Eddie said we'd meet at the Fortress?"

I looked straight ahead. "Ask a lot of questions, don't you?"

"I believe in getting my money's worth. Who is she? An old flame? An old enemy?"

"Yes."

"Is she going to be a problem?"

"Perhaps. We have a history."

Joanna was smiling. Women like to know things like that. "Does she owe you a favour too?"

I sighed, reluctantly realising that Joanna wasn't going to be put off by curt, monosyllabic answers. Some women just have to know everything, even when it's patently none of their business.

"Not so much a favour; more like a bullet in the back of the head. So . . . Suzie Shooter. Also known as Shotgun Suzie, also known as *Oh God, it's her, run!* The only woman ever thrown out of the SAS for unacceptable brutality. Works as a bounty hunter, in and around the Nightside. Probably got paper on someone hiding out in the Fortress."

Joanna was looking at me closely, but I kept on looking straight ahead, my face carefully calm. "All right," she said finally. "Would she be willing to help us?"

"She might. If you can afford her."

"Money is no object, where my daughter is concerned."

I looked at her. "If I'd known that, I'd have charged you more."

She started to laugh, and then it turned into a cough, as she hugged herself hard again. "*Damn,* it's cold! I can hardly feel my fingers. I'll be glad to get back into the light again. Maybe it'll be warmer, out on the street."

I stopped abruptly, and she stopped with me. She was right. It was cold. Unnaturally cold. And we'd been walking for far too long still to be in the alley. We should have reached the street long before this. I looked behind me, and Strangefellow's small neon sign was just a glowing coal in the dark, far away. I looked back at the alley exit, and it was no nearer now than when we'd started. The alley had grown while I was distracted by Joanna's questions. Someone had been playing with the structure of space, stretching the alley . . . the energy drain manifesting as the sudden cold . . . I could feel the trap closing in around me. Now I was looking for it, I could sense magic in the air, crackling like static, stirring the hair on my arms. Everything seemed far away, and what sounds there were came slow and dull, as though we were underwater. Someone had taken control of the space around us, like closing the lid on a box.

And as I looked, six dark silhouettes appeared, blocking the exit to the alley. Dark men in dark suits, waiting for me to come to them.

"Next time you want to pick a fight," Joanna said quietly, "do it on your own time. It would appear Ffinch-Thomas' daddy has sent reinforcements."

I nodded, trying hard not to let my relief show in my face. Of course; Ffinch-Thomas and his threats. Druid magic and city honour. No problem. I could handle half a dozen yuppie Druid wannabes, and send them home crying to their mothers. The alley spell would collapse soon enough, once I shattered their concentrated will with a little practiced brutality. And then a pale ruddy light filled the alley, leaking out of nowhere, illuminating the scene in shades of blood so Someone else could enjoy the show, and for the first time I saw clearly what was waiting for me at the end of the alley. And I was so scared I nearly vomited right there and then.

They stood together, six of them, things that looked like men but were not men. Human in shape, but not in nature, they wore plain black suits, with neat string ties and highly polished shoes, and slouch hats with the brims pulled low, but that was just part of the disguise. Something to help them blend in, so they could walk the streets without people screaming. It worked, until you looked under the brims of their hats, to where their faces should have been. They had no faces. Just utterly blank expanses of skin, from chin to brow. They had no eyes, but they could still see. No ears, but they could hear. No mouths or noses, but then, they didn't need to breathe. There was something uniquely horrid about the sight, an offence against nature and common sense, foul enough to sicken any sane man.

I knew them, from before. They were fast and they were strong, and they never got tired; and once they had been set on your trail they'd track you to Perdition itself and never once falter. I had seen them tear people literally limb from limb, and trample over screaming bodies. Oh yes, I knew them, of old. They moved forward suddenly, calm and unhurried, stepping out in perfect unison, advancing on me in complete silence, with not even the sound of their own footsteps to accompany them.

I made a sound in the back of my throat, the kind of sound a fox makes when it sees the hounds closing in. Or the sound of a man who can't wake up from a nightmare. I was so scared I was shaking, sweat running down my face. My own personal bogeymen, my pursuers since childhood, come for me at last. Joanna saw my fear, and it quickly infected her too. After seeing some of the things I'd taken in my stride, she knew these had to be really bad. She had no idea. Inside, I was screaming. After all the years of running and hiding, they'd finally found me.

And I was going to die hard, and bloody, and people would vomit when they saw what was left of me. I'd seen their work.

I looked back over my shoulder, wondering if I had time to reach Strangefellows. Maybe run through the bar, and out the back, through the old cellars . . . but they were already there. Six more of them, standing together, cutting me off from hope and safety and all chance of escape. I hadn't even sensed them appearing. I'd spent too long in the everyday world. Got soft, and careless. I looked back at the six bearing down on me. I was breathing hard, my hands opening and closing helplessly.

"What . . . what are they?" said Joanna, clinging to my arm with both hands. She was as scared as I was.

"The Harrowing," I said, my voice little more than a whisper. It was an effort to talk. My mouth was painfully dry, my throat closed like there was a hand round it. "The ones who are always looking for me. Death given shape and form, the act of murder made manifest in flesh and blood and bone."

"The bad people Eddie warned you about?"

"No. These are their emissaries. The ones they always send to kill me. Someone has betrayed me. They couldn't have tracked me down this fast, set up so perfect a trap so quickly. Someone told them where and when to find me, the bastards. Someone sold me out. To the Harrowing."

All the time I was babbling, my mind was working furiously. There had to be a way out of this. Had to be. It couldn't all end so simply, so stupidly, with my guts torn out in a grimy back alley in the middle of a nothing case.

"Can you fight them?" said Joanna, her voice high, bordering on the hysterical.

"No. My bag of tricks is pretty much empty, after so long away."

"But you're the hard man, remember!"

"They're harder."

"Can't you just . . . stare them down? Like you did with Ffinch-Thomas?" Her voice broke off sharply. She could see them more clearly now. The Harrowing.

"They don't have any eyes!" I said, hysteria edging into my voice too. "You can't hurt them; they don't feel anything. You can't even kill them; they're not really alive."

I hit my gift for all it was worth. Most of it was still sleeping at the back of my head, unused for five years, but I forced it ruthlessly awake, knowing I'd pay in pain and damage later. If there was a later. I pushed against my limits, scrabbling with my mind at the spell surrounding me, probing it for weaknesses. Front and back were blocked, but maybe the alley walls . . . I can find things, so I tried as hard as I knew how to find a way out of that alley. The alley walls were solid brick, but walls can conceal a lot of things, in the Nightside. And sure enough my third eye, my private eye, found the outlines of an old door hidden underneath the bricks and mortar of the present wall. A door in the space currently occupied by the right-hand wall, hidden from all but those with a very special gift. From the look of it, the door hadn't been opened in a long time, but its temporal inertia was no match for my desperation. I hit it with all my mind, and space shuddered.

The Harrowing lifted their heads slightly, together, sensing something. I hit the door again and it groaned, springing open just a crack. Bright light flared around the edges of the door, spilling into the alley, pushing back the unnatural bloody light. It was sunlight, pure and uncorrupted, and the Harrowing flinched back from it, just a little. I could hear a wind blowing beyond the door, harsh and ragged, and it sounded like freedom.

"What is that?" said Joanna.

"Our way out." My voice was firmer. "Lots of weak spots and fracture lines in the Nightside, if you know where to look. Come on. We are out of here."

"I can't."

"What?"

"I can't move!" I looked at her. She wasn't kidding. Her face was white as a skull, her eyes as wide as an animal's in a slaughterhouse. Her hands gripped my arm with painful pressure. "I'm scared,

John! They scare me. I can't . . . I can't move. I can't breathe. I can't think!"

She was panicking, lost to hysteria. The Nightside had finally pushed her too far. I'd seen it before. I had to act for us. I hauled her towards the door I'd opened, but her legs wouldn't cooperate, and she fell awkwardly, sprawling across the cobbles and almost dragging me down with her. I forced her hands off my arm, and she curled up on the ground, crying helplessly and shaking all over. I looked at the door, and then at the approaching Harrowing. It was so far, and they were so close. I couldn't drag her. But I could get away. I could still reach the door, force it open, fall through and slam it shut behind me, and be safe. But that would mean leaving Joanna behind. The Harrowing would kill her. Horribly. Partly because they never leave witnesses, and partly as a message to me, and others. They'd done it before.

She was nothing to me. Joanna bloody Barrett, all money and pride and snotty manners, dragging me back into the Nightside against my better judgement. Making me feel sorry for her, and her stupid bloody daughter. I owed her nothing. Nothing worth putting my life at risk, trying to save her. She couldn't run. She fell. She brought it on herself. All I had to do was leave her to the Harrowing, and I'd be safe.

I turned towards the door in the wall, and let go of my hold on it. The door slammed shut in a moment, the daylight snapped off, and the awful ruddy light took back its hold on the alley. I moved back to stand over Joanna, my hands balled into fists. She might not be a friend, or even an ally, but she was a client. I've failed myself more times than I care to remember, but I've always done my best never to fail a client. A man has to have some self-respect.

I threw aside the last of my pride and let out one last, desperate mental call for help. Not many would care, even if they heard, not in the Nightside, but Alex might hear . . . and do something. But even as I opened up my mind, the thoughts of the Harrowing crashed in on me; a deafening cacophony of alien, yammering voices, utterly inhuman, trying to fill my head and force out my own thoughts. I had to shut my mind down again, in self-defence. There wasn't going to be any help—no cavalry, no last-minute rescue. As always, I was all alone, in the night that never ends. Just me, and my enemies, at my throat at last.

The Harrowing closed in, six before and six behind, taking their time now they knew I had nowhere to go. They moved in silence, like ghosts or shadows, or deadly thoughts, and their blank faces were scarier than any murderous expressions could ever have been. Their purpose and intent were clear in their movements—sharp, economic, perfectly synchronised. Not graceful; that was too human an attribute for them. I raised my fists in one last gesture of defiance, and they held up their pale hands. For the first time I saw that their long slender fingers ended in hypodermic needles, protruding inches beyond their nail-less tips. Long slender needles, dripping a pale green liquid. That was new, something I'd never seen before. And I knew suddenly, on a level deeper than instinct, and more sure, that the game had changed while I was away. They weren't here to kill me. They were here to jab me with those needles, drug me till I couldn't fight any more, and then drag me away to . . . somewhere else. To their mysterious, unknown masters. The *bad* people.

I could have cried. I wasn't even going to be allowed the dignity of a quick, if nasty, death. My enemies had something slower, more lingering, planned for me. Torture, horror, madness; perhaps to make me one of them, to do their bidding. Saying their words, carrying out their commands, while some small part of me screamed helplessly, forever trapped and suffering behind my own eyes. I'd rather die. I was finally so scared I got angry. To hell with that, and to hell with them. If I couldn't escape, I could at least defy them. Make them kill me, and deny them their victory, or triumph.

And who knew; if I could hold them off long enough, maybe I'd find some way out of this mess, after all. Miracles do happen, sometimes, in the Nightside.

The first of the Harrowing came in reach, and I hit it right in its blank face, putting all my strength behind the blow. My fist sank deeply into its head, square in the middle where its nose should have been, the pale flesh *giving* unnaturally, stretching like dough. The skin clung stickily to my hand as I jerked it free, and the creature barely swayed under the impact. I spun round quickly, striking out at the others as they came crowding in around me. They were fast, but I was faster. They were strong, but I was desperate. I held them off for a while with sheer fury, but it was like hitting corpses. Their bodies were horribly yielding, as though there was really nothing inside them, and perhaps there wasn't. They were just vessels for my enemies' hatred. They absorbed punishment as a passing thing, of no importance at all, and came back for more. Their hands came at me from all directions, striking like snakes, trying over and over again to catch me with their needled fingers. They had the mindless tenacity of machines, and all I could do was keep moving, keep dodging, getting a little slower with every panting breath. Their needles ripped open my trench coat, and pale green liquid stained the material. I actually got mad enough to pick one of the things up, and throw it back against a wall; but though it hit hard enough to break the bones of a living man, the Harrowing just flattened slightly against the brickwork, like a horrid toy that wouldn't break, and came back at me again.

Faceless, remorseless, completely silent. It was like fighting nightmares. I yelled to Joanna to run, while they were still preoccupied with me, but she just lay huddled on the ground, mouth slack with shock, staring with wide, almost mindless eyes. The Harrowing were all over me by then, and I was so tired, so cold. The best I could do was fool them into working against each other, so that they stabbed each other rather than me. Even rage and terror can only keep you going for so long, and what strength I had left was fast fading away. I was working on how best to make them kill me, when the shadow came moving among them, and everything changed.

The Harrowing's heads all turned at once, as they suddenly realised they weren't alone. Something new had come into the alley, something scarier and even more dangerous than they were. They could feel it, the way predators can always sense a rival. They forgot all about me for the moment, and I collapsed gratefully onto the cobbles beside Joanna, my heart hammering painfully in my chest as I fought for breath. Joanna threw her arms about me, and clung to me, shuddering, hiding her face in my neck. I watched it all.

The Harrowing looked about them, all their blank faces moving as one. They were confused, disoriented. This wasn't in the plan. And then one of the faces was suddenly different from all the others. A long red line had appeared, crossing the empty face where the eyes should have been, immediately leaking blood. The creature hesitantly raised a needled hand to its bloody face, as though to examine the cut.

A shadow swept across the Harrowing, fast as a fleeting thought, and the hand toppled from the wrist and fell away, neatly severed. Blood pumped out of the stump into the chill air, steaming thickly. And I smiled, a nasty gloating smile, as I realised just who had come to my rescue. It was already over. The Harrowing were all finished. They just didn't know it yet.

Something moved among the blank-faced figures, too fast to be seen. Blood flew on the air, spurting from a hundred wounds at once. The Harrowing tried to fight, but all they struck was each other. They tried to run, but wherever they went the shadow was already there before them, cutting and slicing at them, ripping them apart, tearing them to pieces. They couldn't scream, but I like to think that in their last few moments of existence they knew something of the horror and suffering they had always brought to others.

In a matter of seconds, it was all over. The dozen Harrowing, the deadly hounds on my trail, were no more. They had been rendered into hundreds, maybe thousands, of small scattered body parts, spread the length of the alley. Some of them were still twitching. The grimy brick walls ran red with blood, and the cobbled ground was slick with it, save for a small empty circle around Joanna and myself. And a dozen featureless faces, expertly skinned from featureless heads, had been nailed to the wall in neat rows beside the closed steel door leading to Strangefellows.

The bloody light snapped off, and the alley returned to its usual gloom. The bitter chill slowly began to relax its hold. I murmured comfortingly to Joanna, until her death grip on me began to relax, and then I nodded to the still, quiet figure standing beneath the small neon sign.

"Thanks, Eddie."

Razor Eddie smiled faintly, his hands thrust into the pockets of his oversized grey coat. There wasn't a speck of blood on him.

"That's your favour paid off, John."

Something about the way he said that made a lot of things fall into place for me. "You knew this was going to happen!"

"Of course."

"Why didn't you wade in sooner?"

"Because I wanted to see if you still had it."

"You could at least have said something! Why couldn't you have warned me?"

"Because you wouldn't have listened. Because I wanted to send the Harrowing's bosses a warning. And because I do so hate to be indebted to anyone."

And I knew, then. "You told them I was going to be here."

"Welcome back, John. The old place hasn't been the same without you."

Something moved like a fleeting shadow, or a

passing breeze, and there was no-one standing beneath the neon sign. The alley was empty, apart from all the scattered body parts, and the blood sliding down the walls. I should have known. Everyone has their own agenda, in the Nightside. Joanna raised her pale face to look at me.

"Is it over?"

"Yes. It's over."

"I'm sorry. I know I should have run. But I was so *scared*. I've never been that scared before."

"It's all right," I said. "Not everyone can swim when they're thrown in the deep end. Nothing in your old life could ever have prepared you for the Harrowing."

"I always thought I could cope with anything," she said quietly. "I've always had to be hard—to be a fighter—to protect my interests, and those of my child. I knew the game, how it was played. How to use . . . what I have, to get my own way, do all the other people down. But this . . . this is beyond me. I feel like a child again. Lost. Helpless. Vulnerable."

"The rules aren't that different," I said, after a while. "It's still all about the powerful, getting away with murder because they can. And a few of us who won't be beaten down. Fighting our corner, helping those we can, because we must."

"My hero," said Joanna, smiling slightly for the first time.

"I'm no hero," I said, very definitely. "I just find

things. I'm not here to clean up the Nightside. It's too big, and I'm too small. I'm just one man, using what gifts I have to help my clients, because everyone should have someone to turn to, in time of need."

"I never met a man I respected," said Joanna. "Before now. You could have run and left me. Saved yourself. But you didn't. My hero."

She raised her mouth to mine, and after a moment, we kissed. She was warm and comforting in my arms, pressing against my body, and for the first time in a long time, I felt alive again. For a time, I was happy. It was like waking up in a foreign country. Afterwards, we sat there on the bloody cobbles for a while, holding each other. And nothing else mattered at all.

SIX

Storming the Fortress

I hailed a horse and carriage to take us to the Fortress. It was too damned far to walk, especially after that business outside Strangefellows, and I felt in distinct need of a bit of a sit-down. And it was probably a good idea to get my face off the streets for a while. The horse came trotting over, glaring down any traffic that looked like getting in his way. He was a huge brute of a Clydesdale, white as the moon, with broad shoulders and massive silver-hoofed feet, hauling an ornate nineteenth-century hansom carriage, of dark ebony and sandalwood, with solid brass trimmings. The man sitting up top, wrapped in an old leather duster, was carrying a five-foot-long blunderbuss, its long stock etched with offensive charms and sigils. He looked carefully about him as the horse manoeuvred the carriage in beside Joanna and me, clearly ready to use his huge gun at a moment's notice. Joanna had recovered most of her composure by now, if not all her old arrogance, but she was immediately charmed by the horse. She went immediately over to him, to pat his shoulder and rub his nose. The horse whinnied appreciatively.

"What a wonderful animal," said Joanna, almost cooing. "Do you think he'd like some sugar, or a sweetie?"

"No thanks, lady," said the horse. "Gives me cavities. And I hate going to the dentist. Wouldn't say no to a carrot, mind, if you had such a thing about your person."

Joanna blinked a few times, and then looked at me accusingly. "You do this to me deliberately. Every time I think I'm finally getting my head round the Nightside, you spring something like this on me. I swear, my nerves are sitting in a corner, crying their eyes out." She looked back at the horse. "Sorry. No carrots."

"Then get in the carriage and stop wasting my time," said the horse. "Time is money, in this business, and I've got payments to make."

"Excuse me," said Joanna, diffidently, "but am I to understand that this . . . is your carriage? You're in charge here?"

"Damn right," said the horse. "Why not? I do all the hard work. Out in all weathers, wearing grooves in my shoulders from this bloody harness. And I know every road, route, and resurfaced bypass in the Nightside, plus a whole bunch of short cuts that aren't on anybody's maps. You name it, and I can get you there, and faster than any damned cab."

"And the . . . gentleman up top?" said Joanna.

"Old Henry? He's just there to take the fares, make change, and ride shotgun. No-one messes with us, unless they fancy going home with their lungs in a bucket. Handy things, hands. Once I've paid off the bank, I'm thinking about investing in some cybernetic arms. If only so I can scratch my own damned nose. Now are we going to stand around talking all night, for which I charge extra, or are we actually going somewhere?"

"You know the Fortress?" I said.

"Oh sure. No problem. Though I think I'll drop you off at the end of the block. Never know when

"I don't like cabs," I said, just to make conversation while Joanna got her mental breath back. "You never know who they're really working for, or who they're reporting back to. And the drivers always want to talk politics. The few horse and carriage outfits working the Nightside are strictly independent. Horses are stubborn that way. You might have noticed Old Henry doesn't even have any reins; the horse makes all the decisions. Besides, Old Henry probably needs both hands free to handle that massive shooting iron of his."

"Why does he need a gun?" said Joanna, her voice back to normal.

"Keeps the other traffic at bay. Not everything that looks like a car is a car. And you never know when the trolls are going to take up carjacking again."

"I feel a distinct need to change the subject," said Joanna. "Tell me more about this Suzie Shooter we might be running into at the Fortress. She sounds . . . fascinating."

of gun known to man, as well as a few she's had made up specially, but mostly she favours the pump-action shotgun. You can usually tell where she's been, because it's on fire. And you can track her down by following the kicked-in doors, scattered screaming and blood splashed up the walls. Her presence can start a fight, or stop one dead. Hell of a woman."

"Were you ever . . . close? You said you had a history . . ."

"We worked some cases together, but Suzie doesn't let anyone get close. I don't think she knows how. Men have been known to enter her life from time to time, but they usually exit running."

"Razor Eddie, Shotgun Suzie . . . you know the most *interesting* people, John. Don't you know any ordinary people?"

"Ordinary people don't tend to last long, in the Nightside."

"Is she likely to be a help, or a hindrance?"

"Hard to tell," I said honestly. "Suzie's not the easiest of people to work with, especially if you prefer to bring your quarry back alive. Suzie's a killer. She only became a bounty hunter because it provides her with a mostly legal excuse for shooting lots of people."

"But you like her, don't you? I can hear it in your voice."

"She's been through a lot. Endured things that would have broken a lesser person. I admire her."

"Do you trust her?"

I smiled briefly. "You can't trust anyone here. You should know that by now."

She nodded. "Razor Eddie."

"And he's my friend. Mostly."

We spent the rest of the ride in silence. We both had a lot to think about. Joanna spent a lot of the time looking out the window. I didn't. I'd seen it all before. The carriage finally lurched to a halt, and the horse yelled back that we'd reached our destination. I got out first, and paid Old Henry, while Joanna got her first look at the Fortress. (I made sure Old Henry got a good tip, one he'd remember. Never know when you might need a ride in a hurry.) The horse waited till Old Henry nodded that everything was okay, and then he set off again. I went over to Joanna, who was still staring at the Fortress. It was worth looking at. Hadn't changed a bit in five years.

The Fortress started out life as a discount warehouse. Stack them high, sell them cheap, and absolutely no refunds. It dealt mostly in weapons, from all times and places, no questions asked, but it made the mistake of flooding the market. Even in the Nightside, there are only so many people who need killing at any given time. So the warehouse tried quietly instigating a few turf wars, to stimulate demand, and that was when the Authorities took an interest.

Next day the property was up for sale. The alien abductees took it over, lock, stock and a whole lot of gun barrels.

The Fortress was a squarish building of several storeys, with all its windows and doors protected behind reinforced steel shutters. There were heavy-duty gun emplacements on the flat roof, looking up as well as down, and all kinds of electronic gear. No-one ever approached the Fortress without being carefully scrutinised well in advance. The word *FORTRESS* had been painted in big letters across the front wall, over and over, in every language under the sun, and a few spoken only in the Nightside. They weren't hiding. They're proud of what they are. The Fortress is still primarily a last refuge for alien abductees, but it was there for anyone in need, for short-term stays. They'd provide counseling, another address more suited to your needs, and whatever kind of weapons you needed to make you feel safe. The Fortress firmly believed in the *Kill them all and let God sort them out* school of therapy. Being abducted from the age of ten will do that to you. Those few people stupid enough to abuse the Fortress's hospitality never lived long enough to boast about it.

The Fortress stood between a Voodoo Business School and an Army Surplus Store. Joanna just had to stop and look in the windows. The Voodoo establishment's current display boasted St. John The Conqueror's Root in easy-to-swallow capsules, Mandrake

Roots with screaming human faces, and a Pick & Mix section of assorted charms. They'd dressed up a window dummy as Baron Samedi, complete with mock graveyard, but it looked more tacky than anything.

The Army Surplus window had uniforms from throughout history, a display of medals from countries that didn't exist any more, and a single executive's suitcase, closed, marked *Backpack nuke; make us an offer.* Joanna looked at that for a long time, before turning to me.

"Are they *serious*? Could that actually be the real thing?"

"Must be something wrong with it," I said. "Otherwise, the Fortress would have bought it. Maybe you have to supply your own plutonium."

"Jesus wept," said Joanna.

"He did indeed," I agreed. "And over worse things than this."

We approached the Fortress's front door, and that was when I first got the feeling that something was seriously wrong. The security camera over the door had been smashed, and the reinforced steel door was standing slightly ajar. I frowned. That door was never left open. Never. I stopped Joanna with a gentle pressure on her arm, gestured for her to be quiet and stay well behind me, and then I carefully pushed the door open a way. From inside came the faint sounds of distant gun-fire and the occasional scream. I smiled briefly.

"Looks like Suzie's here. Stick close to me, Joanna, and try to look harmless."

I pushed the door all the way open and looked in. The lobby was deserted. I walked in, very quietly, and studied the situation carefully.

The lobby had probably been very comfortable originally, designed to put new visitors at their ease, but now it was just a mess. All the up-to-the-moment furniture had been overturned, the country-side scenes on the walls hung crookedly, punctured with bullet holes, and the tall rubber plant in the corner had been riddled with extremely unfriendly fire. Normally you had to pass through a bulky ex-airport metal detector to get into the lobby proper. Someone had thrown it half-way across the room. There was still some smoke drifting on the air, and the unmistakable smell of cordite. Someone had let off a whole lot of rounds in here, and pretty damned recently at that.

But there weren't any bodies, anywhere.

I slowly crossed the lobby, Joanna sticking as close to me as she could without actually climbing into my pockets. I checked out the security cameras in the ceiling corners. The little red lights showed they were still operating. Someone had to have seen what went down here, but there was no sign of any reinforcements. Which could only mean the real action was still going on, somewhere deeper inside the building. I was beginning to get a really bad feeling.

The door on the other side of the lobby, that gave access to the inner layers of the Fortress, was also standing ajar. All its locks and bolts had been smashed, and one of the door's hinges had been torn clean away from the door-jamb. I carefully pushed the door aside and peered out into the corridor beyond. There were fresh bullet scars on the walls, but still no bodies. From further ahead came the sound of multiple gun-shots and angry shouting.

"Maybe we should nip next door to the Army Surplus and pick up some guns of our own?" said Joanna.

"Would you know how to use one, if we did?"

"Yes."

I looked at her. "You're just full of surprises, aren't you? I don't like guns. They make it too easy to make the kind of mistakes you can't put right by saying 'Sorry' afterwards. Besides, I've never felt the need."

"What about the Harrowing?"

"Guns wouldn't have stopped them anyway."

Joanna gestured at the cameras up by the corridor ceiling. "Why all the security?"

"Abductee logic. They have cameras in every room, every corridor, every nook and cranny. And more hidden booby-traps than I feel comfortable thinking about. And, a whole team of people whose only job is to sit and watch the monitors, in shifts. These people are genuinely afraid that the aliens will come for them again. And since no-one knows how the little grey bastards come and go, the cameras are always running. The idea is, that while human eyes might be fooled, cameras would still catch them. I suppose once the security team spots them, they hit every alarm in sight, and everyone grabs the nearest weapon and shoots the shit out of anything that doesn't look entirely human. They even have cameras in the toilets and showers, just in case. No-one here is being taken again without one hell of a fight first."

Joanna pulled a face. "No privacy anywhere? *Seriously* paranoid."

"Not if They really are after you. And the more I look at what's happened here . . . the less I like it. All the signs are that someone, or something, crashed into the lobby, and the Fortress people opened fire. To no obvious effect. From the sound of it, they're still fighting, but they're clearly on the retreat. Something is pushing them further and further back, into the heart of their own territory. So far, so obvious. But, where are the bodies? Maybe, just maybe . . . the aliens have come at last, looking for their missing specimens . . ."

"Are you serious?" said Joanna. "*Aliens?*"

I looked down the empty corridor, considering the possibilities. "All sorts end up in the Nightside. Past, present and future. Aliens are no stranger than a lot of the things I've seen here."

"Maybe we should come back another time," said Joanna.

"No. These are good people. I can't walk away, when they might need help. I never could. And Suzie's probably in there somewhere . . . Damn. *Damn.* I really didn't need this right now. You can wait outside if you want, while I check this out."

"No. I feel safer with you, wherever you are. My hero."

We shared a quick smile, and then I led the way down the corridor. The sound of gun-fire slowly grew louder, along with incoherent shouting and cursing. Lots more structural damage along the way, but still no bodies. Not even any blood. Which, given the sheer amount of gun-fire, was disturbing . . . The corridor ended in a sharp right turn. We were right on top of the fire-fight now. I made sure Joanna was standing well back, and then peered quickly round the corner. Whereupon everything became extremely clear. I should have known. I sighed deeply, and stepped round the corner and into clear view. I raised my voice, cold and commanding and really annoyed.

"Everybody cut it out, right now!"

The shooting stopped immediately. Silence fell across the corridor before me. Smoke curled thickly on the still air. At the far end of the corridor, a whole crowd of people were sheltering behind furniture they'd dragged out of adjoining rooms to pile into a barricade. I counted at least twenty different kinds of guns protruding through the improvised barricade before I gave up. Most of them looked to be full automatic. And facing them, at my end of the corridor, was a tall blonde in black leathers, with a pump-action shotgun in her hands, kneeling behind her own improvised barricade. She looked back at me and nodded briskly.

"John. Heard you were back. Be with you in a minute, soon as I've dealt with this bunch of self-abuse experts."

"Put your gun down, Suzie," I said sternly. "I mean it. No more shooting from anyone. Or I am going to get seriously cranky with everyone. Suddenly and violently and all over the place."

"Oh hell," said a voice from behind the far barricade. "As if things weren't bad enough, now John Taylor's here. I could spit. All right, which of you idiots upset *him*?"

Suzie Shooter stood up and snarled at me. She had to be in her late twenties now, and still looked good enough to eat. If you didn't mind a meal that would very definitely bite back. As always, Suzie was dressed in black motorcycle leathers, adorned with steel chains and studs, and two bandoliers of bullets crossing her impressive chest. Knee-length leather boots with steel toe-caps completed the look. Suzie had seen *Girl on a Motorcycle* and *Easy Rider* more times than was healthy, and loved every Hell's Angels movie Roger Corman ever made.

She had a striking face, with a strong bone struc-ture, ending in a determined jaw, and she kept her shoulder-length straw-blonde hair back out of her face with a leather headband supposedly fashioned from the hide of the first man she'd killed. When she was twelve. Her eyes were a very dark blue, cold and unwavering, and her tightly pursed mouth rarely re-laxed into a smile, except in the midst of mayhem and bloodshed, where she felt most at home. She'd never been known to suffer fools gladly, spent her money as fast as it came in, and in general kicked arse with vim and enthusiasm. She liked to say she had no friends and her enemies were dead, but a few people have been known to sneak their way into her life, almost despite her. I, for my sins, was one of them.

Standing there, set against the curling smoke and swaying lights of the corridor, she looked like a Valkyrie from Hell.

"Let me guess," I said, just a little tiredly. "You smashed your way in, demanded they turn your bounty over to you, and when they declined, you de-clared war. Right?"

"I have serious paper on this guy," said Suzie. "And they were very rude to me."

I considered the matter. "I'm sure they're very sorry. Well, try not to kill them all, Suzie. I need someone alive and mostly intact to answer a few questions."

"Hey! Hold everything!" said the voice from behind the far barricade. "It's possible . . . we may have been a bit hasty. Nobody here wants to take on Shotgun Suzie and John bloody Taylor unless it's absolutely necessary. Can't we talk about this?"

I looked at Suzie, who shrugged. "All they have to do is hand over my bounty, and I'm out of here."

"If we hand him over, you'll kill him," said the voice. "He came to us for sanctuary."

"The man has a point," I said. "You do tend towards bringing them in dead, rather than alive."

"Less paperwork," said Suzie.

I looked down the corridor at the twenty or so guns facing me. "If Suzie really wanted you dead, you'd be dead by now. She's given you every chance. I really think you should consider surrendering."

"We guarantee the safety of people who come here," the voice said stubbornly. "That's who we are. Why we are. We're willing to discuss a deal, but we won't betray our principles."

I looked at Suzie. "What poor soul are you after, this time?"

"No-one important. Just some scumbag lawyer who grabbed a client's settlement money and did a runner with it. Five million pounds, and change. I'm down for ten per cent of whatever I recover."

"A *lawyer*?" said the voice. "Oh hell, why didn't you say? If we'd known he was one of them, we'd have given him to you."

I smiled at Suzie. "Another triumph for common sense and diplomacy in action. You see how easy it is, if you just try a little reason first?"

Suzie growled, lowering her shotgun for the first time. "I hate being reasonable. It's bad for my reputation."

I turned back to the far barricade, so she wouldn't see me smile. "I'm here looking for a teenage runaway, name of Cathy Barrett. Who may have got herself into more trouble than she realises. Name ring any bells?"

"I'm not coming out while Suzie's still there," said the voice from behind the barricade.

"You don't have to come out," I said patiently. "Just answer the question. Unless you want me to get a bit peeved with you too."

"Cathy was here," the voice said quickly, "but she took off, a week or so back. Said something was calling to her. Something wonderful. We all tried to talk her out of it, but she wouldn't listen. And this isn't a prison, so . . . She said something about Blaiston Street. And that's all I know."

"Thank you," I said. "You've been very helpful."

"Not like we had much of a choice," said the voice. "Word's already going around about what you did to those poor bastards outside Strangefellows. They're still mopping up the mess."

I just nodded. It wasn't the first time things had been attributed to me that were none of my doing.

Eddie probably started this particular rumour, as a way of saying sorry. It helps to have a reputation for being a bit of a bastard. People will believe anything of you.

"I'll leave you and Suzie to sort this out between you," I said. "Just give her everything she asks for, and you shouldn't have any more problems with her."

"Thanks a whole bunch," said the voice bitterly. "I think I'd rather face the aliens again."

I gestured for Suzie to step around the corner for a moment, so we could talk privately. I introduced her to Joanna, and the two women smiled at each other. I just knew they weren't going to get on.

"So," said Suzie, "found another lost lamb to look after, have you, John?"

"It's a living," I said. "Been a while, Suzie."

"Five years, three months. I always knew you'd come crawling back to me someday."

"Sorry, Suzie. I'm only here because I'm working a case. Soon as I find my runaway, I'm out of here. Back to the safe, sane, everyday world."

She stepped forward, fixing me with her wild, serious gaze. "You'll never fit in there, John. You belong here. With the rest of us monsters."

I didn't have an answer for that, so Joanna stepped into the silence. "What, precisely, is your connection with John, Miss Shooter?"

Suzie snorted, loudly. "I shot him once, but he got

over it. Paper I had on him turned out to be fake.
We've worked together, on and off. Good man in a
tight corner. And he always leads me where the action is. The real action. Never a dull moment, when
John's around."

"Is that all there is to your life?" said Joanna. "Violence, and killing?"

"It's enough," said Suzie.

I decided the conversation had gone about as far
as it was safe for it to go, and turned to Joanna. "I
know Blaiston Street. Not far from here. Bad neigh-
bourhood, even for the Nightside. If Cathy has gone
to ground there, the sooner we find her, the better."

"Need any help?" said Suzie.

I looked at her thoughtfully. "Wouldn't say no, if
you're offering. You busy?"

She shrugged. "Things have been quiet recently. I
hate quiet. Just let me finish up here and collect what
I'm owed, and I'll catch up with you. Usual fee?"

"Sure," I said. "My client's good for it."

Suzie looked at Joanna. "She'd better be."

Joanna started to say something, noticed that
Suzie's shotgun was pointing right at her, and very
sensibly decided not to take offence. She ostentatiously turned her back on Suzie, and fixed her attention on me.

"At least now we've got an address. What are the
odds Cathy could have got into serious trouble
there?"

"Hard to say, without knowing what drew her there. I wouldn't have thought there was anything on Blaiston Street to attract anyone. There isn't anywhere lower, except maybe the sewers. It's where you end up when you can't fall any further. Unless things have changed dramatically, since I was away. Suzie?"

She shook her head. "Still a snake pit. If you burned the street down, the whole city would smell better."

"Don't worry," I said quickly to Joanna. "She's your daughter. You said yourself she can look after herself. And we're right on her heels now."

"Don't put money on it," said Joanna, the corners of her mouth turning down. "Cathy's always been good at giving people the slip."

"Not people like us," I said confidently.

"There are no people like us," said Suzie Shooter.

"Thank God," said the voice from behind the far barricade.

SEVEN

Where the Really Wild Things Are

Joanna and I left Suzie Shooter intimidating the entire Fortress through the sheer force of her appalling personality, and headed for Blaiston Street. Where the wild things are. Every city has at least one area where all the rules have broken down, where humanity comes and goes, and civilisation is a sometime thing. Blaiston Street is the kind of area where no-one has ever paid any rent, where even the little comforts of life go only to the strongest, and plague rats go around in pairs because they're frightened. It's mob rule, on the few occasions when the brutal inhabitants can get their act together long enough to form a mob. They live in the dark because they like it that way. Because that way they can't see how far they've fallen. Drink, drugs and despair are the order of the day on Blaiston Street, and no-one ends up there by accident. Which made Cathy's choice of destination all the more disturbing. What on earth, or under it, could have called a vital, mostly sensible young girl like her to such a place?

What did she think was waiting for her there?

It was raining, soft pitterpatters of blood temperature that made the streets glisten with the illusion of freshness. The air was heavy with the smell of restaurants, of cuisines from a hundred times and places, not all of them especially appealing. The ever-present neon seemed subtly out of focus behind the rain, and the people passing by had hungry, angry faces. The Nightside was getting into its stride.

"This is a hell of a place," Joanna said abruptly.

"Sometimes literally," I said. "But it has its attractions. Just as it's always the bad boy that makes the good girl's heart beat that little bit faster, so it's the darker pleasures that seduce us out of the everyday world, and into the Nightside."

Joanna snorted. "I always thought you could find every kind of pleasure in London. I've seen the postcards in public phone kiosks, advertising perversion at reasonable rates. Every kind of sex, with and without bodily contact, performed by people of every kind of sex. And a few proudly in between. Pre-op, post-op, during the op . . . I mean, what's left?"

"Trust me," I said seriously. "You really don't want to know. Now change the subject."

"All right. What was it like, growing up here, in the Nightside?" Joanna looked at me earnestly. "This must have been . . . an unusual place, for a child."

I shrugged. "It was all I knew. When miracles and wonders happen every day, they lose their powers to amaze. This is a magical place, in every sense of the word, and if nothing else, growing up here was never boring. Always some new trouble to get into, and what more could a curious child ask for? And it's a great place to learn self-discipline. When they tell you to behave or the bogeyman will get you, they aren't necessarily kidding here. You either learn to be a survivor early on, or you don't get to grow up. You can't trust anyone to watch your back for you . . . not friends or family. But there's an honesty to that, at least.

"This all seems normal to me, Joanna. Your world, the calm and reasonable, mostly logical, everyday London　　　a revelation to me. Safe, sane, reassuringly　　　　　. . . There's a deal of comfort in b　　　　　nymous, of knowing that some-　　　　*happen*, with no great signifi-　　　　se. The Nightside is lousy　　　　and intrusions and inter-　　　　d Below. But though your　　　　e and protected, it's also . . .　　　　loody hard to earn a living in. I'll

　　　her, she climbed in, somewhat dazed. I got in beside her, slammed the door, and we were off. The seats were red leather, and very comfortable. Not a lot of room, but cosy. It was a smooth ride, which argued for some fairly sophisticated springs somewhere down below.

go back there, when I'm through with this case, but I couldn't honestly say whether that's because I prefer it, or because I've lost my touch in how to survive in a place of gods and monsters."

"This Blaiston Street," said Joanna. "It sounds a dangerous location, even for the Nightside. Are you sure Cathy was heading there?"

I stopped, and she stopped with me. It was a question I'd been asking myself. The voice at the Fortress might have said anything, just to get rid of us, and get Suzie off his back. I would have. But . . . it was my only lead. I scowled, frustrated, and the people passing by gave us a little more room. I've always been able to find anything with my gift. That was how I'd made my reputation. To be back in the Nightside, and blind in my private eye, was almost too much to bear. I ought to be able to pick up at least a glimpse of her, if she really was so close, on Blaiston Street.

I lashed out with my mind, hitting the night like a hammer-blow, forcing my gift out across the secret terrains of the hidden world. It beat on the air, wild and angry, pushing open locked doors with grim abandon, and people around me clutched their heads, cried out and shrank away. My hands closed into fists at my sides, and I could feel myself smiling that old vicious smile, that wolf on a trail smile, from a time when nothing mattered but getting to the truth. There was a sick, vicious pain throbbing in my left temple. I could do myself some serious damage by forcing my gift beyond its natural limits, after so long asleep, but right then I was so angry and frustrated I didn't care.

I could feel her out there, Cathy, not long gone, her traces still vibrating on the membrane of the hidden world, but it was like reaching out for something you can sense in the dark, but not see. Someone, some thing, didn't want me to see her. My smile widened nastily. Hell with that. I pushed harder, and it was like slamming my mind against a barbed-wire fence. Blood was dripping steadily from my left nostril now, and I couldn't feel my hands. Serious damage. And then some tension, some defence, broke under my determination, and Cathy's ghost sprang into being before me. It was a recent image, a manifestation only days old, shimmering right there on the street before me. I grabbed Joanna's hand so she could see it too. Cathy hurried down the street, really striding out, and we hurried after her. Her face sparkled and shimmered, but there was no mistaking the broad smile on her face. She was listening to something only she could hear, something *wonderful*, that called to the very heart of her, and it was drawing her in like an angler plays a fish, leading her straight to Blaiston Street. The smile was the most terrible thing. I couldn't think of anything in my life I'd ever wanted as much as Cathy clearly wanted what the unheard voice was promising her.

"Something's calling her," said Joanna, gripping my hand so hard it hurt.

"Summoning her," I said. "Like the Sirens called the Greek sailors of old. It could be a lie, but it might not. This is the Nightside, after all. What disturbs the hell out of me is that I can't even sense the shape of whatever it is that's out there. As far as my gift's concerned, there's nothing there, never has been. Nothing at all. Which implies major shields, and really heavy-duty magic. But something that powerful should have showed up on everyone's radar the moment it appeared in the Nightside. The whole place should be buzzing with the news. A new major player could upset everyone's apple carts. But no one knows it's here . . . except me. And I'm damned if I can even guess what anything that powerful would want with a teenage runaway."

Cathy's ghost snapped out, despite everything I could do to hang on to it. My gift retreated back into my head and slammed the door shut after it. The headache was really bad now, and for a moment all I could do was stand there in the middle of the pavement, eyes clenched shut, fighting to hold my thoughts together. When this case was finally over, I was going to need some serious healing time. I opened my eyes and Joanna offered me a handkerchief, gesturing at my nose. I dabbed at my left nostril until the bleeding finally gave up. I hadn't even felt her let go of my hand. I was pushing myself way too hard, for my first time back. Joanna stood close to me, trying to comfort me with her presence. The headache quickly faded away. I gave Joanna her bloodied handkerchief back, she received it with a certain dignity, and we set off towards Blaiston Street again. I didn't mention my lapse, and neither did she.

"Is Suzie really as dangerous as everyone seems to think she is?" said Joanna, after a while, just to be saying something.

"More, if anything," I said honestly. "She built her reputation on the bodies of her enemies, and a complete willingness to take risks even Norse berserkers would have balked at. Suzie doesn't know the meaning of the word *fear*. Other concepts she has trouble grasping are *restraint, mercy* and *self-preservation*."

Joanna had to laugh. "Damn it, John; don't you know any normal people here?"

I laughed a little myself. "There are no normal people here. Normal people would have more sense than to stick around in a place like this."

We walked on, and though people were giving me plenty of room, no-one even glanced at me. Privacy is greatly valued in the Nightside, if only because so many of us have so much to hide. The traffic roared past, never stopping, rarely slowing, always in such a hurry to be somewhere else, to be doing something somebody else would be sure to disapprove of. There are no traffic lights in the Nightside. No-one would pay them any attention anyway. There are no official

street crossings, either. You get to the other side of
the street through courage and resolve and intimidating the traffic to get out of your way. Though I'm told
bribery is also pretty effective. I looked at Joanna,
and asked her a question I'd been putting off for too
long. Now we were finally getting close to Cathy, I
felt I needed to know the answer.

"You said this wasn't the first time Cathy ran
away. Why does she keep running away, Joanna?"

"I try to spend time with her," said Joanna, looking straight ahead. "Quality time, when I can. But it
isn't always possible. I lead a very busy life. I work
all the hours God sends, just to stay in one place. It's
ten times harder for a woman than a man, to get
ahead and stay ahead in the business world. The people I have to deal with every day would eat sharks for
breakfast, as an appetizer, and have turned betrayal
and back-stabbing into a fine art. I work bloody hard,
for the security Cathy takes for granted, to get the
money to pay for all the things she just has to have.
Though Heaven forfend she should show the slightest interest in the business that makes her comfortable world possible."

"Do you enjoy your work?"

"Sometimes."

"Ever thought about trying something else?"

"It's what I'm good at," she said, and I had to nod.
I knew all about that.

"No stepfathers?" I said casually. "Or father figures? Someone else she could turn to, talk to?"

"Hell, no. I swore I'd never make the mistake of being tied to a man again," Joanna said fiercely. "Not after what Cathy's father put me through, just because he thought he could. I'm my own woman now, and whoever comes into my life does so on my terms. Not a lot of men can cope with that. And I have trouble hanging on to the few that can. The work, again. Still, Cathy never wanted for anything she really needed. I raised her to be bright, and sharp, and independent."

"Even from you?" I said quietly. Joanna wouldn't even look at me.

And that was when the world suddenly changed. The living city disappeared, and abruptly we were somewhere else. Somewhere much worse. Joanna and I stumbled on for a few steps, caught off guard, and then we stopped and looked quickly about us. The street was empty of people and the road was empty of traffic. Most of the buildings surrounding us were nothing more than ruins and rubble. The taller buildings had apparently collapsed, long ago, and everywhere I looked nothing was more than a storey or two high. I could see for miles now, all the way to the horizon, and it was all destruction and devastation. I turned in a slow circle, and everywhere was the same. We had come to a dead place. London, the Nightside, the old city, was now a thing of the past. Something bad had come, and stamped it all flat.

It was very dark now, with all the street-lights and the glaring neon gone. What light there was had a dull, purple cast, as though the night itself was bruised. It was hard to make out anything clearly. There were shadows everywhere, very deep and very dark. Not a normal light to be seen anywhere, in any of the wrecked and tumbledown buildings; not even the flicker of a camp-fire. We were all alone, in the night. Joanna fumbled in her bag and finally produced her cigarette lighter. Her hands shook so much it took her half a dozen goes to get it to light. The warm yellow flame seemed out of place in such a night, and the glow didn't travel far. She held the lighter up high as we looked around, trying to get some sense of where we were, although I already had a sinking feeling I knew what had happened.

It was quiet. Very quiet. No sounds at all, save for the shuffling of our feet and our own unsteady breathing. Such utter quiet was eerie, unsettling. The roar of the city was gone, along with its inhabitants. London had been silenced, the hard way. I only had to look around in the awful purple light to know that we had come to an empty place. The heavy silence was almost overpowering, until I felt like shouting out . . . something, just to emphasize my presence. But I didn't. There might have been something listening. Even worse, there might not.

I'd never felt so alone in my life.

All around us the buildings were squat, deformed, their shapes altered and the edges softened by exposure to wind and rain. Long exposure. All the windows were empty, every trace of glass gone, and I couldn't see a single doorway with a door; just dark openings, like eyes or mouths, or maybe wounds. There was something almost unbearably sad in seeing such a mighty city brought so low. All those centuries of building and expanding, all those many lives supporting and giving it purpose, all for nothing, in the end. I moved slowly forward, and puffs of dust sprang up around my feet. Joanna made a noise at the back of her throat and moved slowly after me.

It was cold. Stark and bitter cold, as though all the heat had gone out of the world. The air was still, with not even a breath of wind blowing. Our footsteps seemed very loud in the quiet, loud and carrying as we walked down the middle of what had once been a street, through what had once been a vital, thriving place. We were both shivering now, and it had nothing to do with the cold. This was a bad place, and we didn't belong here. Off in the distance, broken buildings stood blackly against the horizon in jagged silhouettes, shadows of what they had once been. The city, inside and out, was over.

"Where are we?" Joanna said finally. The hand holding up the lighter was steadier now, but her voice trembled. I didn't blame her.

"Not . . . where," I said. "When. This is the future. The far future, by the look of it. London has fallen, and civilisation has come and gone. This isn't even an epilogue. Someone closed the book on London and the Nightside, and closed it hard. We've stumbled into a Timeslip. An enclosed area where Time can jump back and forth, into the past and the future and everything in between. Needless to say, there wasn't a Timeslip here the last time I came this way. Anyone with two brain cells to rub together knows enough to avoid Timeslips, and they're always well sign-posted. If only because they're such arbitrary things. No-one understands how they work, or even what causes them. They come and they go, and so do whatever poor bastards get sucked up in them."

"You mean we're trapped here?"

"Not necessarily. I've been using my gift to try and find us a way out. The physical area of a Timeslip isn't very large. If I can just locate the boundaries, crack open a weak spot . . ."

"Not very large!" Joanna's voice rose, harsh with emotion. "I can see for miles, all the way to the horizon! It'll take us weeks to walk out of here!"

"Things aren't always as they appear. You should know that by now." I kept my voice calm and light, trying to sound knowledgeable and reassuring, and not at all as though I was just guessing. "While we're in the Timeslip, we see all of it; but the actual affected area is comparatively small. Once I can crack a hole in the boundary, and we walk through, we'll snap back to our own time. And I'd say we're only half an hour away. Easy walk. Assuming, of course, that nothing goes wrong."

"Wrong?" said Joanna, seizing on the word. "What could possibly go wrong? We're all alone here. This is the far future, and everyone's dead. Can't you feel it? The lights of London have finally gone out . . ."

"Nothing lasts forever," I said. "Everything comes to an end, in Time. Even the Nightside, I suppose. Let enough centuries pass, and even the greatest of monuments will fall."

"Maybe they dropped the Bomb, after all."

"No. The Nightside would survive the Bomb, I think. Whatever did happen here . . . was much more final."

"I hate to see London like this," Joanna said quietly. "It was always so *alive*. I always thought it would go on forever. That we built it so well, ran it so tightly, loved it so much, that London would outlast us all. I guess I was wrong. We all were."

"Maybe we just went away and built another London somewhere else," I said. "And as long as people are around, we'll always need a Nightside, or something like it."

"And what if people aren't around, any longer? Who knows how far into the future we are now? Centuries? Millennia? Look at this place! It's dead.

It's all dead. Everything ends. Even us." She shuddered abruptly, and then glared at me, as though it was all my fault. "Nothing's ever easy around you, is it? A Timeslip . . . Is this sort of thing usual, in the Nightside?"

"Well," I said carefully, "it's not unusual."

"Typical," said Joanna. "You can't even trust *Time* in the Nightside."

I couldn't argue with that, so I looked around me some more. Millennia? The ruins looked old, but surely not that old. "I wonder where everyone is. Did they just up and leave, when they saw the city was doomed? And if so, where did they go?"

"Maybe everyone's gone to the moon. Like in the song."

That was when I finally looked up, and the chill sank past my bones and into my soul. It was suddenly, horribly, clear why it was so dark. There was no moon. It was gone. The great swollen orb that had dominated the Nightside sky for as long as anyone could remember was missing from the dark sky. Most of the stars were gone too. Only a handful still remained, scattered in ones and twos across the great black expanse, shining only dimly, a few last sentinels of light against the fall of night. And since the stars are so very far away, perhaps they were gone too, and this was just the last of their light to reach us . . .

How could the stars be gone? What the hell had happened . . .

"I always thought the moon seemed so much bigger in the Nightside because it was so much closer here," I said finally. "Perhaps . . . it finally fell. Dear Jesus, how far forward have we come?"

"If the stars are gone," Joanna said softly, "do you suppose our sun has gone out too?"

"I don't know what to think . . ."

"But . . ."

"We're wasting time," I said roughly. "Asking questions we have no way of answering. It doesn't matter. We're not staying. I've got the far boundary fixed in my head. I'm taking you there, and we are getting the hell out of here, and back to where we belong."

"Wait a minute," said Joanna. "The *far* boundary? Why can't we just turn around and go back the way we came, through the door that brought us here?"

"It's not that simple," I said. "Once a Timeslip has established itself, nothing less than an edict from the Courts of the Holy is going to shift it. It's here for the duration. If we go back, we'll just re-emerge by the Fortress again, and the Timeslip will still be between us and Blaiston Street. We'd have to go around the Timeslip to reach Blaiston Street, and for that we'll need a fairly major player to map the Timeslip's extent and affected area. Or we'll just keep ending up here again."

"How long could such a mapping take?"

"Good question. Even if we could find someone powerful enough who wouldn't charge us an arm and a leg, and could fit it into his schedule straight-away . . . we're talking days, maybe even weeks."

"How big could a Timeslip be?"

"Another good question. Maybe miles."

"That's ridiculous," said Joanna. "There must be another way of reaching Blaiston Street!"

I shook my head reluctantly. "The Timeslip's connected to Blaiston Street, on some level. I can feel it. Which makes me think this can't be coincidental. Someone, or something, is protecting its territory. It doesn't want us interfering. No. Our best bet is to cross this space to the far boundary, where I can force an opening, and we should emerge right next to Blaiston Street. Shouldn't be too difficult. This is all pretty unpleasant, but I don't see any obvious dangers. Just stick with me. My gift will guide us right there."

Joanna looked at me, and I looked back, trying hard to seem confident. Truth be told, I was just winging it, going by my guts and my instincts. In the end, she looked away first, staring unhappily about her.

"I hate this place," she said flatly. "We don't belong here. No-one does, any more. But Cathy's been gone too long already, so . . . Which way?"

I pointed straight ahead, and we set off together.

Joanna held her lighter out before her, but the yellow glow didn't travel far at all. The small flame stood still and upright, untroubled by even the slightest murmur of breeze. I tried not to think about how much longer it would last. The purple light around us seemed even darker in comparison. I was feeling colder all the time, as though the empty night was leeching all the human warmth out of me. I would have improvised a rough torch of some kind, but I hadn't seen any wood anywhere. Just bricks and rubble, and the endless dust.

The quiet was getting on my nerves. It just wasn't natural, to be so completely quiet. This was the quiet of the tomb. Of the grave. It had an almost anticipatory quality, as though somewhere off in the darkest and deepest of the shadows, *something* was watching, and waiting, and biding its time to attack. The city might be empty, but that didn't mean the night was. I was reminded suddenly of how I'd felt as a small child, when my father would put me to bed at night and turn out the light. Back when he still cared enough, and was sober enough, to do such things. Children know the secret of the dark. They know it has monsters in it, which might or might not choose to reveal themselves. Now here we were, in the darkest night of all; and more and more I was convinced something was watching us. There are always monsters. That's the first thing you learn, in the Nightside.

Some of them look just like you and me.

Perhaps the monster here was London itself. The dead city, resenting the return of the living. Or maybe the monster was just loneliness. A man and a woman, in a place that life had left behind. Man isn't meant to be alone.

Our footsteps seemed to grow louder and more carrying as we made our way down what had once been a main street. The dust should have absorbed the sound. There was enough of it. It was everywhere, thick layers of it, undisturbed for God alone knew how long. It was at its worst in the street, but we'd learned the hard way that we had no choice but to stick to the very middle of the street. Buildings had a tendency to collapse, if we got too close. Just the vibrations of our tread were enough to disturb their precarious rest, and whole sections of wall would crumble and fall away, crashing to the ground in great angry clouds of the grey dust. I picked up one brick, and it fell apart in my hand. I tried to work out how ancient it must be, to have become so delicate, but the answers I came up with made no sense. The human mind isn't comfortable with numbers that big.

Just when I thought I was finally coming to terms with where and when I was, things got worse. I started hearing things. Sounds, noises, so faint at first I thought I'd imagined them. But soon they were coming from all around us, from before and behind, subtle, disturbing sounds that seemed to be gradually creeping closer. I don't have that good an imagination. The sounds were almost familiar, but not quite, giving them a strange, sinister feel. And all the time, drawing gradually, remorselessly, closer. I didn't turn my head, but my eyes probed every shadow as I approached it. Nothing. I increased our pace, and the sounds kept right up with me. Following us, tracking us, keeping their distance for the moment, but never too far away. My hands were sweating now. Clattering, chattering noises, that I could almost put a name to. Joanna had picked up on them too, and was glaring openly about her. The flame in the lighter flickered so wildly I was afraid it would go out, and I put a hand on her arm, ostensibly to slow our pace again.

"What the hell is *that*?" she said fiercely. "Could there be something here with us, after all? Something alive?"

"I don't know. But the sound's coming from a lot of directions at once, which suggests that there's a lot of them, and they're all around us." I glared at the shadows from which the ruins grew, but I couldn't make out a damned thing. Anything could have been hiding in there. Anything at all. I was getting less happy by the minute. "Whatever they are, they seem to be content for the moment to keep their distance. Could be they're more afraid of us than we are of them."

"Don't take bets on it," said Joanna. "How much further to the boundary?"

I checked with my gift. "Half an hour's walk. Maybe half that, if we run. But running might send the wrong message."

She looked at me abruptly. "Could it be the Harrowing, after you again?"

I shook my head firmly. "Not so soon after Razor Eddie's little message. Whoever's behind the Harrowing will want to consider the ramifications of that for a while. I would. Even the major players can get really twitchy whenever Razor Eddie's name comes up. Besides, the Harrowing have never been able to track me that accurately. Or I wouldn't have survived this long. Maybe . . . it's insects. I always thought that if anything would outlast Humanity, it would be the bloody insects. Scientists were always saying the damn things would be the only creatures to survive a nuclear war. It could well be insects. *Damn*. I hate creepy-crawlies."

"You're sure it couldn't be anything human? Maybe some other poor soul who got sucked into the Timeslip, maybe hurt and trapped and trying to get our attention?"

I scowled. I should have thought of that. Unlikely, but . . . I sent my gift out into the night, trying to find the source of the sounds, and to my astonishment I locked on to a human trace straightaway. We had to be right on top of him.

"There is someone here! A man . . . one man, on his own. Not moving. Could be hurt . . . this way."

I ran down the street, clouds of dust billowing up around my pounding feet, Joanna right there at my side. I was starting to get used to that. I kind of liked it. We lost track of the sounds around us, caught up in the excitement of finding another human being alive in this awful, dead place. Could be a visitor, could be a survivor . . . could be the answer to a whole lot of questions. And it could be just some poor soul who needed help. First things first. My gift tracked his location as accurately as any radar, leading us off the main street and down a side alley. We slowed to a walk immediately, for fear our footsteps would bring down the brick walls on either side of the alley. But the walls stood firm, not even trembling as we passed.

Finally, we came to a halt beside a large ragged hole in the left-hand wall. The jagged edges of the hole made it seem . . . organic, more like a wound than an entrance. I prodded a protruding brick with a careful fingertip, but it didn't crumble at my touch. Odd. It was very dark beyond the hole, and the air had a faint but distinct mouldy smell. I gestured for Joanna to hold her lighter closer, but the light didn't penetrate more than an inch or two.

"He's in *there*?" said Joanna. "Are you sure? It's pitch-black . . . and I can't hear anything."

"He's in there," I said firmly. "My gift is never

wrong about such things. But it does feel . . . odd." I put my head cautiously into the hole. "Hello? Can you hear me? Hello!"

We waited, but there was no reply. The brickwork didn't even shudder at the vibrations of my raised voice. As I listened, I realised the faint sounds that had been following us had stopped. I told myself we'd left them behind, but I wasn't convinced. I pulled my head back and studied the hole in the wall. The more I looked at the situation, the less I liked it. The whole thing smelled of a trap, with the (possibly) injured man as bait. There could be anything waiting in the darkness beyond the hole. But there was definitely a man in there, even if he wasn't answering, and if he was hurt . . . we could be his only chance. And I was damned if I'd abandon anyone here in this Godforsaken place. So . . . I took a deep breath, the smell of mould tickling my nostrils and the back of my throat, and then I eased myself cautiously through the hole in the wall. It was a tight fit. I found the floor with my foot and stepped into the utter darkness of the room beyond. I stood very still for a long moment, listening, but there was no reaction anywhere. I stepped aside, and Joanna followed me in, bringing the feeble yellow light with her.

It looked like two rooms had been knocked through into one, and pretty messily at that. There were dark objects all over the floor. They didn't look like bricks, but I didn't feel like touching them to find out what they were, so I stepped carefully round them as I moved further into the room. The air was close and foul, dry and acrid, but with an underlying scent of decay, as though something had died here, not that long ago. There was no dust on the floor, but the bare brick walls were thick with ugly mounds of grey furry mould. I kept moving, following my gift, Joanna holding her lighter out before us. Shadows danced menacingly around us. It soon became clear we were heading for the far corner, occupied by what seemed to be a huge, dirty grey cocoon. It filled the corner from floor to ceiling; nine feet tall and three feet wide. I thought about what kind of insect might emerge from a cocoon of such size, and then decided very firmly that I wasn't going to think about that any more. *Hate* creepy-crawlies. I kept looking around for the subject of our search, but he was nowhere to be seen, despite my gift urging me forward.

Until finally we were standing right in front of the cocoon, glistening palely in the glow from the lighter, and there was nowhere else to go.

"Tell me you're not thinking what I'm thinking," said Joanna.

"He's in there," I said reluctantly. "He's still alive. Alive, and in there . . . because there's nowhere else he can be."

I swallowed hard, and reached out one hand to the cocoon. The material was hot and sweaty to the touch, something like silk, something like spiderweb, and my flesh crawled instinctively just at the feel of it. I grabbed a handful at about head height, and tore it away by brute strength. The horrid stuff clung stickily to my fingers, stretching unnaturally rather than breaking, and it took all my strength to open up a hole in the outer layer of the cocoon. There was a face underneath. A human face. The skin was grey, the eyes were closed. I hesitated, sure he must be dead, even though my gift was never wrong, and then the eyelids quivered, as though the eyes were trying to open.

I thrust both hands into the hole I'd made and tore the material away from his face. It fought me, clinging to my fingers and the face, trying to repair the broken threads even as I tore them apart. I yelled for Joanna to help, and between us we broke open a larger gap, freeing the head and shoulders. I pulled the last of the stuff away from the face, the eyes finally opened, and I was forced to admit that I knew the face. It was older than I remembered, and much more lined, and the eyes held more horror than I ever want to think about, but it was still, clearly, Razor Eddie.

His eyes slowly came into focus as they looked at me. I scrubbed the last sticky traces from his face with Joanna's handkerchief. The eyes were aware, but that was all. There was no recognition in them, no sense of self, of humanity. Joanna and I talked

loudly and comfortingly as we forced open the cocoon, splitting it apart inch by inch, until finally we
had an opening large enough to drag him out of. His
whole body was limp, unresponsive. He was wearing
his old grey coat, even more of a mess than I remembered, much holed and tattered, soaked with
slime and darkened with what looked like a whole lot
of bloodstains.

We hauled him away from the cocoon, but his legs
wouldn't work, so we had to lower him to the floor
and set him down with his back against the wall to
support him. He was breathing heavily now, great
gasping breaths, as though he wasn't used to it. I
didn't even want to guess how long he'd been in the
cocoon, or what it had done to him. I had a hundred
questions, but I kept talking calmly, trying to reach
Eddie, bring him up out of the place he'd had to hide
in, deep inside himself, for the sake of his own sanity. His eyes fixed on me, ignoring Joanna.

"It's all right, Eddie," I said. "It's me. John Taylor.
You're out of that . . . thing. You get your strength
back, and your legs working, and we'll get you out of
here and back to the Nightside. Eddie? Can you hear
me, Eddie?"

A slow knowledge came into his unblinking eyes,
though the horror never quite left them. His mouth
worked slowly. I leaned closer, to hear his quiet
voice. It was rough and harsh, and painful, as though
he hadn't used it in a long, long time.

"John . . . Taylor. After all this time. You . . . bastard. God damn you to Hell."

"What?" I jerked back, shocked, sure he must have misunderstood. "I'm going to get you out of here, Eddie. It's going to be all right."

"It'll never be all right . . . Never again. This is all your fault. All of this."

"Eddie . . ."

"I should have killed you . . . when I had the chance. Before you . . . destroyed us all."

"What are you talking about?" Joanna said angrily. "We only just got here! He hasn't done anything! This is a Timeslip!"

"Then damn you, John . . . for what you will do."

"You're blaming me for this?" I said slowly. "You're blaming me . . . for something I haven't even done yet? Eddie, you must know I'd never do anything to bring the world to this. The end of everything. Not by choice, anyway. You have to tell me. Tell me what to do, to prevent this happening."

Razor Eddie's mouth moved in a slow, utterly mirthless smile. "Kill yourself."

"You betrayed John to the Harrowing," said Joanna. "Why should we believe anything you say? Maybe we should forget about rescuing you. Just stick you back in the cocoon again."

"That's not going to happen, Eddie," I said quickly, as the horror filled his eyes again. "Come with us. Help us prevent this. We're not far from the

Timeslip's boundary. I can crack it open, get us home again. Back where we belong."

"Back . . . into the past?"

That stopped me for a moment. If this Eddie had got here the hard way, the long way, could I risk taking him back? Would the Nightside accept two Razor Eddies? I pushed the thought aside. It didn't matter. There was no way I was going to leave Eddie here. In the dark. In the cocoon. Some things you just can't do and still call yourself a man.

We got him on his feet, and this time his legs supported him. Even after all he'd been through, he was still Razor Eddie, and tough as nails. Joanna and I helped him across the room, pushed and pulled him through the hole in the wall, and out into the alley. As soon as we were all out into the night, the sounds started up again. Eddie actually cringed for a moment as he heard them, but only for a moment. His gaze was steady now, and his mouth was firm. By the time we reached the main street again, he was walking on his own. Something had broken him, something awful, but he was still Razor Eddie.

"How did you end up the only living person here?" I said finally. "*When* is this, anyway? How far in my future? I've just come back into the Nightside, after five years away. Does that help you date it? Dammit, Eddie, how many centuries have passed, since the city fell?"

"Centuries?" said Eddie. "It seems like centuries.

But I've always had a good grasp of time. Not centuries, John. It's only been eighty-two years since you betrayed us all, and the Nightside fell."

Joanna and I looked at each other, and then out over the deserted city. The crumbling buildings, the starless, moonless night.

"How could all this have happened in just eighty-two years?" I said.

"You were very thorough, John. All of this is down to you. Because of what you did." Eddie tried to sound more accusing, but he was just too tired. "All Humanity is dead . . . thanks to you. The world is dead. Cold and corrupt, the only remaining life . . . like maggots writhing in a rotten fruit. And only I am left . . . to tell the tale. Because I can't die. Part of the deal I made . . . all those years ago. On the Street of the Gods. Fool. Damned fool. I have lived long enough . . . to see the end of everything and everyone I ever cared for. To see all my dreams dashed, and made into nightmares. And now I want so badly to die . . . and I can't."

"What did John do?" Joanna said urgently. "What could he have done . . . to bring about this?"

"You should never have gone looking for your mother," said Eddie. "You couldn't cope, with what you found. You couldn't cope with the truth."

"Hang in there, Eddie," I said lamely. "You're going home. Back in Time, to the Nightside as it was.

And I swear to you . . . we'll find a way to prevent this. I'll die, rather than let this happen."

Razor Eddie turned his head away and wouldn't look at me. He breathed deeply of the relatively fresh air, as though it had been a long time since he'd breathed anything like it. He was walking more or less normally now, and we were making a good pace as I headed us towards the boundary. But we were still in the same street when it all went to hell.

They came up out of holes in the ground, before and behind and all around us. Dark and glistening, squeezing and forcing their flexible bodies through the ragged openings in the dusty ground. We stopped dead in our tracks, looking quickly around us. And everywhere there were long spindly legs, hard-shelled bodies, compound eyes, grinding teeth and clattering mandibles, and long, quivering antennae. Insects, of all shapes and breeds, species I'd never seen before, all horribly, unnaturally large. More of them came scuttling and scurrying out of the ruined buildings, or skittering down the crumbling walls, light as a breath of air for all their size, joining the hundreds and hundreds already circling us, hopping and seething in a living carpet, covering the ground. The smallest were six inches long, the largest two and even three feet in length, with great serrated mandibles that looked sharp enough and strong enough to take off a man's arm or leg in a single vicious bite. Sometimes the insects crawled right over each other to get a better look at us, but for the moment at least they maintained a safe distance.

I could feel my gorge rising. I really can't stand creepy-crawlies.

"Well," I made myself say lightly, "I always thought insects would end up inheriting the world. Just never thought they'd be so bloody *big*."

"Cockroaches," said Joanna, her voice thick with loathing and disgust. "Revolting things. I should have stomped on more when I had the chance." She waved her cigarette lighter at the nearest insects, and they actually seemed to shrink back a little. It had to be the light. It wasn't any real threat now, but their instincts remembered. Maybe we could use it to open up a path, make a run for it . . . I glanced at Eddie, to see how he was doing, and was horrified to discover he was quietly crying. What had they *done* to him? The great and terrible Razor Eddie, Punk God of the Straight Razor, reduced to tears by a bunch of bloody bugs? I was suddenly so angry I couldn't speak. Somehow, before I left this place, there was going to be some serious payback.

"This . . . is disgusting," said Joanna. "We've come to where the really wild things are. Nature at its most basic and appalling."

"Got that right," said a familiar, cheerful and self-satisfied voice. I looked round sharply, and there he was, in a little circle entirely clear of insects—the Collector. An old acquaintance of mine, from before

I left the Nightside. Not a friend. I don't think the Collector has friends. Got a hell of a lot of enemies, though. He was currently dressed as a gangster from the Roaring Twenties; every detail correct, from the white spats on his shoes to the overbearing colour scheme of the waistcoat, to the snap-brimmed hat. But he was at least thirty pounds too heavy for the suit, and his stomach strained against the half-buttoned waistcoat. As always there was an impression of the utterly false about him. Of someone hiding behind a whole series of masks. His face was almost painfully florid, his eyes gleamed fiercely, and his smile was totally insincere. No change there, then. Warm yellow sunlight surrounded him, from no obvious source, and the insects gave it plenty of room.

"What the hell are you doing here, Collector?" I said. "And who did you steal that incredibly vulgar suit from?"

"It is rather good, isn't it?" said the Collector smugly. "It's an original Al Capone, acquired from his very own wardrobe when he wasn't looking. He won't miss it. He had twenty others just like it. I even have a letter of authentification, from Capone's tailor." He beamed about him, not in the least disturbed by his surroundings. "We do meet in the strangest places, don't we, John?"

"Do I take it you know this person?" said Joanna, looking at me almost accusingly.

"This is the Collector," I explained resignedly.

"You name it and he collects it; even if it's nailed down and surrounded by barbed wire. Nothing too rare or too obscure but he hasn't got a line on it. He has an endless appetite for the unique item, and the thrill of the chase. Word is he gets off just indexing his hoard. The Collector, thief, con man, cheat, and quite possibly the most conscienceless individual in the Nightside. There's nothing he won't go after, no matter how precious it might be to other people. I know other collectors, not in his league, who'd give everything they owned, and everything you owned, just for a tour of the Collector's famous and very well hidden warehouse. How's it going, Collector? Found the Phoenix's Egg yet?"

He shrugged. "Hard to tell, until it hatches." He turned his entirely unconvincing smile on Joanna. "You don't want to believe everything you hear about me, my dear. I am a very misunderstood man."

"No you're not," I said. "You're a grave robber, a miser and a meddler in history. Archaeologists use your name to frighten their children. You don't care who gets hurt, as long as you get what you want."

"I save things that would otherwise disappear into the mists of history," said the Collector, unperturbed. "One day I'll open a museum in the Nightside, so everyone can appreciate my treasures . . . But for the moment there are just too many competitors, jealous people, who would cheerfully rob me blind."

"What are you doing here, Collector?" I said. "I

wouldn't have thought there was anything valuable left here for you to appropriate."

"You have such limited vision, John," said the Collector, shaking his head sadly. "Surrounded by treasures, and so blind to them. Look around you. There are species of insect here unknown to the world we came from. Unique variations, unavailable anywhere else. I know collectors who speculate in insects who will piss blood when they hear what I've got. I'll take back a few duplicates, of course, to auction off for utterly extortionate prices. Travelling in Time can be so expensive these days."

"Time travel?" Joanna said quickly. "You have a time machine?"

"Nothing so crude," said the Collector. "Though I do have rather a nice display of some of the more rococo mechanisms . . . No, I have a gift. Many do, in the Nightside. Dear John here finds things, Eddie kills with a razor that no-one ever sees . . . and I flit back and forth in Time. It's how I've been able to acquire so many lovely pieces. But to answer your next question; no, I don't carry passengers. How did you get here, John?"

"Timeslip," I said. "I was heading for the boundary when these insects appeared. When exactly are you from, Collector?"

"You've just left the Nightside," said the Collector. "In something of a hurry, swearing never to return. Do I take it you're back?"

"Five years up the line, after you left," I said. "I'm back, and my mood has not improved."

"Can't say I'm surprised," said the Collector. He grinned happily about him. "Ah, so many beauties, I don't know where to start. I can't wait to get them back to my warehouse and start pinning them to display boards!"

Joanna snorted. "Hope you brought a really big killing bottle."

The insects were stirring restlessly all around us, antennae twitching with dangerous agitation. I decided to get to the point. "Collector, Eddie says we're only eighty-two years in my future, but everything here is destroyed. Do you know what brought this about?"

The Collector spread his fat, nail-bitten hands in an innocent gesture. "There are so many futures, so many possible timelines. This is just one possibility. If it's any comfort, there's nothing inevitable about this."

"You knew this future well enough for your gift to bring you here," I said. "You knew about the insects. Talk to me, Collector. Before I get upset with you."

The Collector just kept on smiling his insufferable self-satisfied smile. "You're in no position to make threats, John. In fact, you don't even recognise just how much danger you're in. You're right; I have studied these insects, from a safe distance. I know why they're so interested in us. In humans. I even know why they haven't just killed you. I'm afraid it's rather an unpleasant reason, but then, that's insects for you. Such wonderfully uncluttered minds. No room for fear, or other emotions. They don't even bother with sentience, as we understand it. They're concerned only with survival. I've always admired their ruthlessness. Their single-minded, implacable nature."

"You always were strange," I said. "Get to the point." It seemed to me that the insects around us were edging closer.

"You never studied," said the Collector. "Insects lay their eggs in host bodies. Non-insect host bodies. The eggs grow and hatch inside the host, and the larvae then eat their way out. A bit hard on the host, of course, but . . . Nasty, totally without conscience and compassion, and utterly insect. However, the only living species left in this future world are insects. So all they've got left to use for a host is . . . that unfortunate fellow with you. For eighty-two years now, the undying form of Razor Eddie has been host to generation after generation of insects. Eggs go in, larvae with teeth come out, and the insect race survives. Rather unpleasant for poor Eddie, of course, eaten alive over and over again, but then . . . I never liked him."

I didn't look at Eddie. He didn't need to see my shock and horror at what had been done to him. Especially if it really was my fault. I knew now why the insects had kept him imprisoned in a cocoon. They couldn't risk his finding a way to kill himself. I was so angry then . . . if I'd been big enough, I'd have stamped on every damned insect in the world.

"And now here you are, John," said the Collector. "You and your lady friend. New hosts, for more insect young. I shouldn't think you'll last anywhere near as long as Eddie, but I'm sure they'll make good use of you, while you do last. I suppose I could help you escape . . . but then, I never liked you much either, John."

Razor Eddie cried out suddenly, his back arching, his whole body shaking and shuddering. I grabbed him by the shoulders, but his spasms were so violent I couldn't hold on to him. He fell to the ground, gritting his teeth to keep from crying out again, but his eyes were leaking tears in spite of him. I knelt beside him. I think I already knew what was happening. I didn't back away as hundreds of insect young the size of thumbs burst out of his flesh, eating their way out of his convulsing body. Black soft squishy things, with teeth like tiny razors. They even came out through his eyes. His coat soaked up most of the blood. Joanna fell to one knee and vomited, but still managed to hang on to her lighter. I grabbed handfuls of the emerging larve and crushed them viciously. Their innards ran down my wrists, but there were just too many of them.

"What can I do, Eddie?" I said desperately, but he couldn't hear me.

"Only one thing you can do," the Collector said reasonably. "Kill him. Put him out of his long misery. Except, of course, you can't. This is after all the re- markable Razor Eddie, who cannot die. Take a good look at him, John. Once that cigarette lighter runs out of fuel, they'll come for you . . . and this will be your future, and hers, for as long as they can make you last . . ."

I pushed his hateful words aside, concentrating on my gift. If there was anything that could still kill Razor Eddie, and give him peace at last, my gift would find it. It didn't take long. Pretty obvious, once I had the answer. The only thing that could kill Eddie was his own straight razor. The weapon that no-one ever saw. I already knew it wouldn't be any- where about his person, or he'd have used it on him- self before now. The insects couldn't separate him from it, either. Eddie and his Razor were bound to- gether by a pact only a god could break. I focused my gift further, and there it was, in the one place the insects could put it that Eddie couldn't reach it. They'd buried it deep inside his own body, in his guts.

I made myself act without thinking, without feel- ing. I thrust my hand into one of the insects' exit wounds, forcing it open, and then drove my hand deep into Eddie's guts, not listening as he screamed, holding him down with all my weight as he kicked. Joanna was dry-heaving by now, but she couldn't bring herself to look away. My arm was bloody up to the elbow by the time my fingers closed around the pearl handle of the old-fashioned straight razor, and Eddie howled like a damned thing as I pulled my hand back out again. Blood dripped thickly from my fingers and my prize. Eddie lay shuddering, moaning quietly. I opened the razor and set the edge against his throat, and I like to think there was gratitude in his eyes.

"Good-bye, Eddie," I said softly. "I'm so sorry. Trust me. I won't let this happen."

"How very sentimental," said the Collector, "but you haven't really thought this through, have you?" I didn't need to look round to know that he was enjoying every moment of this. "You see, if you destroy the insects' only host, and then remove yourself and the woman from this Time, you will be condemning every species here to extinction. Are you really ready to commit genocide, to wipe out the only living things left on the earth?"

"Hell yes," I said, and Razor Eddie didn't even twitch as I cut his throat, pressing down so hard with the blade that I could feel the steel edge grate against his neckbones. I needed to be sure. Blood pumped out under pressure, soaking his clothes and mine, and the dusty ground around us. Eddie lay there peacefully as he died, and afterwards I held him in my arms and cried the tears he couldn't. Because for all our differences, and there had been many, he had always been my friend. When the very last of his life went out of him with a sigh, his razor disappeared from my hand. I lowered his body to the ground and clambered unsteadily to my feet. The Collector was looking at me, utterly stupefied.

"*Hate* creepy-crawlies," I explained.

The insects screamed suddenly; a shrill inhuman sound that filled the purple night. It had taken them a while, but they'd finally understood the significance of what I'd done. The scream rose and rose as more and more of them took it up, until it seemed to be coming from everywhere in the desolate city. I smiled my old smile, my devilish smile, and the Collector flinched at the sight of it. The insects were boiling all around us, pressing right up to the limits of the yellow light. I had just murdered all their future generations . . . unless they could find a way to make use of me, and Joanna. I checked the distance to the far boundary again. Fifteen minutes' running time, maybe ten, depending on how motivated we were. As long as the lighter fuel held out.

The Collector cried out suddenly as holes opened up in the ground around his feet. The insects down below weren't intimidated by his light, and they had finally come for him. One of the Collector's legs plunged down into a gaping hole, and he cried out in pain and shock as unseen jaws sank deep into the meat of his leg. More holes opened up in the ground around me and Joanna, but I had already hauled her to her feet by main force, and we were off and running. We left Eddie's body behind. He was past caring, at last. And already decaying, as the long years finally caught up with him.

We ran past the Collector, who was screaming shrilly as he scrabbled in his suit pockets for something. He finally pulled out a shiny canister, and sprayed the contents down the hole. More of the insects screamed underground, and the Collector was able to pull his leg free. Huge chunks of flesh were missing, the cracked bone clear among red strings of meat. The Collector whimpered, and then sprayed his canister wildly about him as more holes opened up. The light he stood in was flickering unsteadily now as his concentration wavered. He swore briefly, like a disappointed child, and vanished, back into Time. The light snapped off, and the insects charged forward, coming after Joanna and me as we ran for the boundary.

Joanna was back in control again, her face grim and focused as she held the lighter out before her, almost like a cross to ward off the undead. It seemed to me the flame was smaller than it had been, but I didn't say anything. Either it would last, or it wouldn't. Insects crowded in all around us, scrambling over each other in their eagerness to get at us, but still they couldn't bring themselves to enter the gradually shrinking pool of yellow light. There were some the size of dogs, and some the size of pigs, and I hated them all. Joanna and I ran straight at them, and they fell aside at the very last moment, huge dark mandibles snapping shut like bear traps. I glanced again at Joanna's lighter, and didn't like what I saw. The flame wasn't going to last until we reached the boundary, and if it didn't, neither would we. So I called on my gift one more time, to find a path of power.

There are lots of them, in the Nightside, with lots of names; from the uber science of the ley lines to the shimmering magic of the Rainbow Run, there have always been roads of glory, hidden from all but the keenest of gazes, holding the substance of the world together with their immaterial energies. If you had the courage to run them, you could gain your heart's desire. Supposedly. And even now, in this desolate and deserted place, the paths of power remained. My gift locked on to one that led right to the Timeslip boundary, and called it up into existence. A bright, vivid, scintillating path appeared before us, and the insects fell back from the new light as though they'd been burned. Joanna and I ran on, hand in hand, pushing ourselves hard, and sparks flew up from our pounding feet.

But I was already slowing. Using the gift had taken a lot out of me, at the end of a long, hard day. I'd used my gift too often, pushed it too hard, and I

was paying the price now. My head was throbbing so
hard I could barely see anything outside of the path,
and blood ran steadily from both my nostrils and
dripped from my chin. My legs felt very far away.
Joanna was having to drag me along now, keeping
me moving through sheer determination. I could feel
the boundary drawing closer, but it still seemed a hell
of a way off. Like in those dreams where you run as
hard as you can, and still never get anywhere. Joanna
was yelling at me now, but I could hardly hear her.
And the insects were all around us, a scuttling carpet
of dark intent.

I was tired and hurting, but even so I was surprised when my legs just suddenly gave out, and I
fell. I hit the glory path hard, and small shocks ran
through me, none of them enough to get me back on
my feet again. So close, the magic was almost
painful. The insects surged right up to the edge of the
light, staring at me with expressionless compound
eyes. Joanna leaned over me, and tried to raise me
up, but I was too heavy. I rolled over onto my side
and looked up at her.

"Get the hell out of here," I said. "I've taken you
as far as I can. There's nothing more I can do for you.
Boundary's straight ahead. I've already cracked an
opening that will take you back to the Nightside. Go
find your daughter, Joanna. And be kind to her. In
memory of me."

She let go of my arm, and it dropped limply to the bright track. I couldn't even feel it.

"I won't leave you," said Joanna. "I can't just leave you."

"Of course you can. If we both die here, who'll help your daughter? Don't worry; I'll be dead before the insects get to me. I'll see to that. Maybe . . . by dying here, now, I can prevent this ever happening. Time's funny that way, sometimes. Now go. Please."

She stood looking down at me, and suddenly her face was utterly blank. All the emotion had gone out of it. Shell-shocked, again, perhaps. Or just considering the matter. She turned away from me, staring down the glowing path towards a boundary whose existence she could only take on faith. She was going to leave me behind, to die. I could feel it. Part of me cursed her, and part of me urged her on. I'd always known something in the Nightside would kill me, and I hated the thought that I might drag someone else down with me. And then she turned back, all the blankness gone from her face, and she grabbed me by the arm again with both hands.

"Get up!" she said fiercely. "Damn you, get up on your feet, you bastard! We haven't come this far together for you to give up now! I'm not leaving without you, so if you don't get up, you're killing me along with you. So move, damn you!"

"Well," I said, or thought I said. "If you put it that way . . ."

Between the two of us, we got me back on my feet again, and we staggered down the shimmering path. I kept thinking that the next step would be my last, that there just wasn't anything left in me, but Joanna kept me going. Half-supporting, half-carrying me, urging me on with comforting words and shouted obscenities. She dragged me down the path, all the way to the boundary, the insects screaming shrilly all the way, until suddenly we crashed through the crack I'd opened and back into our own Time.

We collapsed together on a rain-slick street, fighting for breath, and the wonderful roar of the living city was all around us. Bright neon and thundering traffic, and people, people everywhere. The night sky was full of the blaze of stars, and the great and glorious moon. It was good to be home. We lay side by side on the pavement, and people walked around us, ignoring the blood that soaked my clothes. The Nightside is a great place for minding your own business. I looked at the moon in its bright unblinking eye, and said sorry. Not everyone gets to see the possible results of their own future actions. The world that could be, if they really screw up. I wondered whether I should tell the present-day Razor Eddie of what I'd seen in the possible future. I thought not. There are some horrors no man should have to contemplate, not even the Punk God of the Straight Razor.

Not every future is etched in stone. I should know.

I'd seen enough, before now. But I still felt guilty, even if I didn't know what for.

You should never have gone looking for your mother. That's what the future Eddie had said. I'd always been curious about the mother who abandoned me. The woman who wasn't actually human after all. In the early hours of the morning, when a man just can't sleep, I'd often wondered if I help other people find things that matter to them because I can't find the one thing that really matters to me. Well, now I'd have something else to think about at three o'clock in the morning.

I looked at Joanna. "You know, I really thought you were going to leave me there, for a moment."

"For a moment," she said slowly, "I was. I surprised myself. I didn't know I had that kind of determination in me." She frowned. "But it was ... strange. Something in me didn't want to help you. Don't ask me to explain, because I can't. It's like there's something on the tip of my tongue, a word or a memory I can't quite grasp ... Oh hell, it doesn't matter. We both got out. Now let's get up off this freezing-wet pavement and go find Blaiston Street. After all we've been through to get there, I'm curious to see what it looks like. It had better be worth it."

"Cathy will be there," I said.

"And we will find her, and save her from whatever damn fool mess she's got herself into this time. Anything else can wait. Right?"

"Right," I said, not entirely sure just what it was I was agreeing to.

When I did find out it was, of course, far too late.

EIGHT

Time Out At the Hawk's Wind Bar & Grill

I'd just seen the end of the world, murdered one of my oldest friends, and discovered that the one quest I'd always intended to give my life to was now forever barred to me; so I decided I was owed a break. Luckily there was a really good café close by, so I took Joanna firmly by the hand and led her there, so that we could both get our mental breath back. The Nightside will grind down the toughest of spirits, if you don't learn to take the occasional pit stop, when you can. Joanna didn't want to go, with Blaiston Street and the answer to her daughter's fate now so close at hand, hopefully, but I insisted. And she must have been tired and shaky too, because she'd actually stopped arguing before we reached our destination.

The Hawk's Wind Bar & Grill is a sight to see, something special even among the Nightside's many dark wonders, and I stopped outside a moment, so Joanna could appreciate it. Unfortunately, she wasn't in the mood. Which was a pity. It's not every day you get to see such a perfect monument to the psychedelic glories of the sixties, complete with rococo Day-Glo neon and Pop Art posters with colours so bright they practically seared themselves onto your retinas. The Hindu latticed doors swung politely open before us as I urged Joanna in, and I breathed deeply of the familiar air of the sixties as we entered the café; joss sticks and patchouli oils, a dozen kinds of smoke, all kinds of freshly brewing coffee, and a few brands of hair oil best forgotten.

The place was packed and jumping, as always, all the hits of the sixties throbbing loudly on the thick air, and I smiled about me at familiar faces as I led Joanna through the maze of tables to find a reasonably private spot at the rear of the café. Strangefellows is where I go to do business, or a little private brooding; Hawk's Wind is where I go for the peace of my soul. Joanna looked disparagingly at the stylised plastic table and chairs, but sat down with a minimum of fuss. I liked to think she was beginning to trust my instincts. Her nostrils twitched suspiciously at the multicultural atmosphere, and I pretended to study the oversized hand-written menu while she looked about her. There was always a lot worth looking at in the Hawk's Wind Bar & Grill.

The decor was mostly flashing lights and psyche-delia, with great swirls of primary colours on the walls, the ceiling and even the floor. A jukebox the size of a Tardis was pumping out an endless stream of hits and classics from the sixties pop scene, blithely ignoring the choices of those stupid enough to put money in it. The Kinks had just finished "Sunny Afternoon," and the Lovin' Spoonful launched into "Daydream." My foot tapped along as I unobtrusively studied Joanna while she studied the faces around her. The tables around us were crowded with travellers from distant lands and times, heroes and villains and everything in between. Plus a special sprinkling of the kind of people who could only ever have felt at home in a place like this. Names and faces, movers and shakers, and all the unusual suspects.

The Sonic Assassin was showing off his new vibragun to the Notting Hill Sorcerer. The timelost Victorian Adventurer was treating his new sixties stripper girlfriend to the very best champagne. The Amber Prince was sitting alone, as usual, trying to remember how he got there. Any number of spies, ostentatiously not noticing each other. And for a wonder, all five Tracy brothers at the same table. While off in a far corner, what looked like the whole damned Cornelius clan were being their usual raucous selves, running up a tab they had no intention of paying. I had to smile. Nothing much ever changed here. Which was, of course, part of the attraction. The Hawk's Wind Bar & Grill was happily and proudly free of the tyranny of passing Time.

In the centre of the great open floor, two go-go dancers dressed in little more than bunches of white feathers were dancing energetically in ornate golden cages, frugging and bobbing their heads for all they were worth. The one in the silver wig winked at me, and I smiled politely back. A waitress came tripping over to our table in eight-inch pink stiletto heels, plastic mini skirt, starched white man's shirt and a positively precarious beehive hairdo. I stood up and peeled off my trench coat, indicating the blood-soaked material, and the waitress nodded brightly.

"Oh sure, JT; anything for you, baby! Welcome back, daddy-o; looking good! You wanna order yet?"

She was chewing gum, and her voice was an irritatingly high-pitched squeal, but there was no denying she was authentic as hell. I sat back down and handed her the menu.

"Two Cokes, please, Veronica. Nothing else. And fast as you can with the coat. I'm in the middle of a case."

"Never knew you when you weren't, dearie. Any messages from the future?"

"Invest in computers."

"Groovy!"

And off she went, swaying on her heels like a ship at sea. Friendly hands reached out to her from all sides, but she avoided them with practised ease and vicious put-downs. A beatnik stood up to recite some poetry, and we all threw things at him. The Animals were singing an uncensored version of "House of the Rising Sun." Try and find that one on a CD compilation. Joanna leaned forward across the plastic table to glare at me.

"Tell me you haven't dragged me into some hideous sixties theme café. I lived through the sixties, and once was more than enough. And we definitely don't have the time to hang around here while they launder your coat! Cathy is close now. I can feel it."

"We could spend a month in here, and not one second would have passed in the street outside," I said calmly. "It's that kind of place. And the laundry here really is something special. They ship your clothes all the way to China and back, and guarantee it'll come back spotless. They could get all the markings out of the Turin Shroud, and add double starch for no extra charge."

"I need a drink," Joanna said heavily. "And not some damned Coke, either."

"Trust me; you're going to love the Cokes they serve here. Because this café isn't a re-creation of the sixties. This is the genuine article."

"Oh bloody hell. Not another Timeslip."

"Not as such . . . The original Hawk's Wind Bar &

Grill was a hang-out for all the great sixties adventurers and cosmic spirits, and much loved in its day, but unfortunately the café burned down in 1970; possibly in self-immolation, as a protest over the Beatles splitting up. It was due to be replaced by some soulless, boring business school, but luckily the café was so fondly remembered by its famous and gifted patrons that it came back, as a ghost. This whole establishment is one big haunting, a deceased building still stubbornly manifesting long after the original was destroyed.

"A ghost café.

"The people, on the other hand, are mostly real. Either Time-tripping in from the sixties, or just getting into the spirit of the thing. The Hawk's Wind is a genius loci for all that was good and great about the Swingingest era of them all. And because the café isn't real, you can order all kinds of things here that haven't existed since the sixties. Ghost food and drink, which as it isn't real, can't affect a real body. The ultimate in slimming diets; and your last chance to wallow in some serious nostalgia. How long has it been since you've tasted a real Coke, Joanna?"

Our waitress was back, bearing two old-fashioned chunky glass bottles with crimped-on caps, balanced expertly on a tin tray decorated with photos of the Monkees. She slammed the crimped tops expertly against the edge of the table. The caps flew through the air, but not one frothy bubble rose above the mouth of the neck. She placed a bottle before each of us, and dipped in curly-wurly plastic straws. She flashed a grin, cracked her gum, and wiggled off while Joanna looked dubiously at the bottle before her.

"I do not need a straw. I am not a child."

"Go with it. It's all part of the experience. This . . . is *real* Coke. The old, sugar-rich, caffeine-heavy, thick syrup and taste-intensive kind you can't get any more; except in certain parts of Mexico, apparently, which just goes to show. Try it, Joanna. Your taste-buds are about to convulse in ecstasy."

She took a sip, and so did I. She took several more, and so did I. And then we both sat back in our plastic chairs, *ooh*ing and *aah*ing appreciatively, while the dark liquid ran through our bodies, jump-starting all our tired systems. *You don't know what you've got till it's gone,* was crooning from the juke-box, and I could only nod in agreement.

"Damn," said Joanna, after a respectful pause. "*Damn.* This *is* the real thing, isn't it? I'd forgotten how good Coke used to be. Is it expensive?"

"Not here," I said. "This is the sixties, remember? They accept coins from all periods here, and IOUs. No-one wants to risk being barred."

Joanna had relaxed a little, but her mouth was still set in a firm line. "This is all very pleasant, John, but I didn't come into the Nightside to be entertained. My daughter is only a few streets away now, according to you. What are we doing here, when we should be rescuing her?"

"We're here because we need to get our breath back. If we're going to venture into Blaiston Street, we're going to have to be fresh, sharp, and have every last one of our wits about us. Or they'll chop us off at the ankles before we even see them coming. Blaiston Street is only a few blocks away, but it's a whole other world. Vicious, violent, and possibly even more dangerous than the place we just left. And yes, I know that makes you even more desperate to go rushing off to save Cathy, but we're going to need to be at the top of our form for this. And remember, Time doesn't pass out there, while we're in here.

"You're holding up really well after all you've been through, Joanna. I'm impressed. Really. But even the sharpest edge will go blunt if you beat it against a brick wall often enough. So I want you to sit here, enjoy your Coke and the surroundings, until we're both ready to take on the Nightside again. You only think you've seen the bad places. You mess up in Blaiston Street and they'll eat you alive. Possibly literally. And I think . . . there are things we need to talk about, you and I, before we go anywhere else."

"Things?" said Joanna, raising a perfect eyebrow.

"There are things about Cathy, and her situation, that need . . . clarifying," I said carefully. "There's more to this than meets the eye. More to this whole situation. I can feel it."

"There are a lot of unanswered questions," said Joanna. "I know that. Who called Cathy here, and why? Why choose her? She's no-one important, except to me. I'm a successful businesswoman, but I don't earn the kind of money that would make kidnap or blackmail attractive. And this is the Nightside. People like me don't matter here. So why pick on Cathy? Just another teenage runaway? If I knew the answers to questions like those, I wouldn't have needed to hire someone like you, would I?"

I nodded slowly, acknowledging the point. Joanna pressed on.

"I don't think we're in here because I need a rest, John. I think this is your rest stop. You've been through a lot too. You killed Razor Eddie. He was your friend, and you killed him."

"I killed him because he was my friend. Because he'd suffered so much. Because it was the only thing left I could do for him. And because I've always been able to do the hard, necessary things."

"Then why are your hands shaking?"

I looked down, and they were. I honestly hadn't noticed. Joanna put one of her hands on top of mine, and the shaking slowly stopped.

"Tell me about Eddie," she said. "Not the Street of the Gods stuff. Tell me about you, and Eddie."

"We worked a lot of cases together," I said, after a while. "Eddie's . . . powerful, but he's not the most subtle of people. There are some problems you can't solve with power, without destroying what you're trying to save. That's when Eddie would turn up at Strangefellows, asking for my help. Not openly, of course. But we'd talk, and eventually the conversation would come around to what was troubling him, and then he and I would go out into the night, and find a way to put things right that didn't involve hitting the problem with a sledgehammer. Or a straight razor.

"And sometimes . . . he'd just appear out of nowhere, to back me up. When I got in over my head."

"This sounds more like partners than friends," said Joanna.

"He's a killer," I said. "Razor Eddie. Punk God of the Straight Razor. These days he kills with good rather than bad intentions, but in the end all he is, is killing. And he wouldn't have it any other way. Hard to get close to a man like that. Someone who's gone much further into the dark than I ever have. But . . . he turned his life around, Joanna. Whatever epiphany he found on the Street of the Gods, he threw aside everything that had ever had power over him, in order to earn redemption. How can you not admire courage like that? If someone like him can change, there's hope for all of us.

"I've tried to be a good friend to him. Tried to steer him towards a different kind of life, where he doesn't have to define who he is by killing. And he . . . listens, when I have bad times, and need someone I can talk to who won't repeat it. He warns people away from me, if he thinks they're a threat. He hurts people, if he thinks they're planning to hurt me. He thinks I don't know that.

"I killed him in the Timeship to put an end to his suffering. I've always been able to bite the bullet, and do what has to be done. I never said it was easy."

"John . . ."

"No. Don't try and bond me with me, Joanna. There's no room in my life for people who can't protect themselves."

"Is that why your only friends are damaged souls like Razor Eddie and Suzie Shooter? Or do you deliberately only befriend people already so preoccupied with their own inner demons that they won't put pressure on you to confront your own? You're afraid, John. Afraid to really open up to anyone, because that would make you vulnerable. This is no way to live, John. Living vicariously through the problems of your clients."

"You don't know me," I said. "Don't you dare think that you know me. I am . . . who I have to be. To survive. I live alone, because I won't risk endangering someone I might care for. And if it's sometimes very cold and very dark where I am; at least when I do go down, I won't drag anyone else with me."

"That's no way to live," said Joanna.

"And you, of course, are the expert on how to run

your life successfully. A mother whose child runs away at every opportunity. Let's talk about some of the questions you have to consider, before we go any further. What if, we finally go to Blaiston Street, find the right house, kick in the door and find that Cathy's actually very happy where she is, thank you? That she's happy and safe and doesn't need rescuing? What if she's found someone or something worth running to, and doesn't want to leave? Stranger things have happened, in the Nightside. Could you turn and walk away, leave her there, after all we've been through to track her down? Or would you insist she come back with you, back to a life you could understand and approve of, where you could keep a watchful eye on her, to ensure she won't grow up to make your mistakes?"

Joanna took her hand away from mine. "If she was genuinely happy . . . I could live with that. You don't last long in the business world if you can't distinguish between the world as it is and the world as you want it to be. What matters is that she's safe. I need to know that. I could always come back and visit."

"All right," I said. "Try this one. What if she is in a bad place, and we haul her out of there, and you take her back home with you? What are you going to do to ensure she won't just run away again, first chance she gets?"

"I don't know," said Joanna, and I had to give her points for honesty. "Hopefully, the fact that I've come this far for her, gone through so much for her . . . will make an impression. Make her see that I do care about her, even if I'm not always very good at showing it. And if nothing else, this whole experience should give us something in common to talk about, for once. We've always found it difficult to talk."

"Or listen. Make time for your daughter, Joanna. I really don't want to have to do this again."

"I had managed to work that out for myself," said Joanna, just a little coldly. "I always thought Cathy had everything she needed. Clearly, I was wrong. My business can survive without me for a while. And if it can't, the hell with it. There are more important things."

I nodded and smiled, and after a moment she smiled back. It wasn't going to be as simple or as easy as that, and both of us knew it, but recognising a problem is at least half-way to solving it. I was pleased at how far she had come. I just hoped she could go the distance. We sipped our Cokes for a while. The Fifth Dimension finished "Aquarius" and went straight into "Let the Sun Shine."

"That future we ended up in," Joanna said, after a while. "It may not be *the* future, or even the most likely, but it was still a bloody frightening one. How could *you* possibly be responsible for destroying the whole damned world? Are you really that powerful?"

"No," I said. "At least, not at present. It's got to be

tied in to what I inherited, or perhaps stand to inherit, from my missing mother. I never knew her. I have no idea who or what she really was. No-one does. My father found out, and the knowledge made him drink himself to death. And this was a man well used and inured to all the worst excesses of the Nightside."

"What did he do here?" said Joanna.

"He worked for the Authorities. The ones who watch over us, whether we like it or not. After my father died, I went through his papers. Hoping to find some kind of legacy, or message, or just an explanation, something to help me understand. I was ten years old, and I still believed in neat answers like that then. But it was all just junk. No diary, no letters, no photos of him and my mother together. Not even a wedding photo. He must have destroyed them all. And the few people who'd known both my parents had vanished long ago. Driven away by . . . many things. None of them turned up for his funeral.

"Over the years, all kinds of people have come up with all kinds of theories as to who and what my mother might have been. Why she appeared out of nowhere, married my father, produced me, and then disappeared again. And why she didn't take me with her. But no-one's ever been able to prove anything out of the ordinary about me, apart from my gift. And gifts are as common as freckles among the sons and daughters of the Nightside."

Joanna frowned suddenly. "On the tube train,

coming here, the Brittle Sisters of the Hive recognised your name. They backed off, rather than upset you. And they asked to be remembered, when you finally came into your kingdom."

I had to smile. "That doesn't necessarily mean anything. In the Nightside, you can never be sure which ugly duckling might grow up to be a beautiful swan, or even a phoenix. So if you're sensible you hedge your bets and back as many horses as possible. And never make an enemy you don't have to."

Joanna leaned forward across the plastic table, pushing her Coke bottle aside so she could stare at me the more fiercely. "And do you still intend to go on looking for your mother, now you know what might happen to the world if you find her?"

"It's a hell of a wake-up call, isn't it? It's certainly given me a lot of food for thought."

"That isn't answering the question."

"I know. Look, I hadn't even intended to stay here, in the Nightside, once this case was over and done with. I left this madhouse five years ago for good reasons, and none of them have changed. But . . . more and more, this dangerous and appalling place feels like home to me. Like I belong here. Your safe and sane everyday world didn't seem to have any place for me. At least here I get the feeling I could do some real good for my clients. That I could . . . make a difference."

"Oh yes," said Joanna. "You could make a hell of a difference here."

I met Joanna's gaze as calmly as I could. "All I can honestly say is this—I really don't care enough about my mother to risk bringing about the future we both saw."

"But that could change."

"Yes. It could. Anything can happen, in the Nightside. Drink your nice Coke, Joanna, and try not to worry about it."

The Crazy World of Arthur Brown was belting out "Fire," by the time Joanna had calmed down enough to ask another question.

"I need you to be straight with me, John. Do you think Cathy is still alive?"

"I have no reason to believe she's not," I said honestly. "We know she was alive very recently. The last image my gift picked up was only a few days old. We know Someone or Something called her into the Nightside, but there's no direct evidence that individual means Cathy any harm. There's no evidence that he doesn't, either, but when you're groping in the dark it's best to be optimistic. As yet, no clear threat or danger has manifested. We have to proceed on the assumption that she's still alive. We have . . . to have hope."

"Hope? Even here?" said Joanna. "In the Nightside?"

"Especially here," I said. This time I put my hand

on hers. Our hands felt good together, natural. "I'll do everything I can for you, Joanna. I won't give up, as long as there's a shred of hope left."

"I know," said Joanna. "You're a good man at heart, John Taylor."

We looked into each other's eyes for a long time, and both of us were smiling. We believed in each other, even if we weren't too sure about ourselves. I knew this wasn't a good idea. *Never get personally involved with a client.* It's written in large capital letters on page one of *How to Be a Private Detective.* Right next to *Get as much cash as you can up front, just in case the cheque bounces,* and *Don't go looking for the Maltese Falcon because it'll all end in tears.* I'm not stupid. I've read Raymond Chandler. But right then, I just didn't care. I did make one last effort, for the good of my soul.

"It's not too late for you to back out," I said. "You've been through enough. Stay here, and let me handle Blaiston Street. You'll be safe here."

"No," Joanna said immediately, pulling her hands away from mine. "I have to do this. I have to be there, when you find . . . what's happened to my daughter. I have to know the truth, and she has to know . . . that I cared enough to come myself. Dammit, John, I've earned the right to be there."

"Yes," I said, quietly proud of her. "You have."

"John Taylor, as I live and breathe," said a cold, cheerful voice. "I really couldn't believe it when they told me you'd showed up again. I thought you had more sense, Taylor."

I knew the voice, and took my time turning around. There aren't many people who can sneak up on me. Sure enough, standing behind me was Walker, large as life and twice as official. Every inch the City Gent, sharp and stylish and sophisticated. Handsome, if a little on the heavy side, with cold eyes and smile and an even colder heart. Had to be in his late forties by now, but you still wouldn't bet on the other guy. People like Walker don't slow down; they just get sneakier. His perfect city suit was expertly cut, and he tipped his bowler hat to Joanna with something very like charm. I glared at him.

"How did you know where to find me, Walker? I didn't know I was coming here till a few minutes ago."

"I know where everyone is, Taylor. You'd do well to remember that."

"John, who is this . . . person?" asked Joanna, and I could have blessed her for the sheer unimpressed indifference in her voice.

"Perhaps you should introduce me to your client," said Walker. "I would so hate for us to start off on the wrong foot."

"Your tie's crooked," said Joanna, and I could have kissed her.

"This is Walker," I said. "If he has a first name, no-one knows it. Probably not even his wife. Ex-

Eton and ex-Guards, because his sort always is. Mentioned in dispatches for being underhanded, treacherous and more dangerous than a shark in a swimming pool. Walker represents the Authorities, here in the Nightside. Don't ask what Authorities, because he doesn't answer questions like that. All that matters is he could have you or me or anyone else dragged off without warning, with no guarantee we'd ever be seen again. Unless he had a use for us. He plays games with people's lives, all in the name of preserving his precious status quo."

"I preserve the balance," Walker said easily, flicking an invisible speck of dust from his impeccable sleeve. "Because someone has to."

"No-one knows who or what Walker reports to, or where his orders come from," I continued, "Government or Church or Army. But in an emergency he has been known to call for backup from any damned force he wants; and they come running every time. His word is law, and he enforces it with whatever measures it takes. Always immaculately turned out, charming in a ruthless kind of way, and never, ever, to be trusted. No-one ever sees him coming. You can never tell when he's going to come strolling out of the shadows with a smile and a quip, to pour oil on troubled waters, or occasionally vice versa.

"He has a gift for getting answers. There aren't many who can say no to him. They say he once made a corpse sit up on an autopsy table and talk with him."

"You flatter me," said Walker.

"You'll notice he's not denying it. Walker can call on powers and dominations, and make them answer to him. He has power, but no accountability. And damn all conscience, either. In a place where the Light and the Dark are more than just aphorisms, Walker remains determinedly grey. Like any good civil servant."

"It's all about duty and responsibility, Taylor," said Walker. "You wouldn't understand."

"Walker disapproves of people like me," I said, smiling coldly. "Rogue agents, individuals who insist on being in charge of their own destinies, and their own souls. He thinks we muddy the waters. It's not often you'll see him out in the open, like this. He much prefers to stay in the shadows, so people can't see him pulling strings. Anyone at all could be working for him, knowingly or unknowingly, doing his bidding, so Walker doesn't have to get his own hands dirty. And of course, if one of his unofficial agents should get killed in the process, well, there are always more where they came from. For Walker the end always justifies the means, because the end is keeping the Nightside and its occupants strictly separate from the everyday world that surrounds it."

Walker bowed his head slightly, as though anticipating applause. "I do so love it when you introduce me, Taylor. You do it so much better than I ever could."

"He's been known to fit up people," I said. The words were coming faster now, as my anger rose. "When he finds it necessary, to throw someone to the wolves. He is much feared, occasionally admired, and practically everyone in the Nightside has tried to kill him, at one time or another. At the end of the day, he goes home to his wife and his family, in the everyday world, and forgets all about the Nightside. We're just a job to him. Personally, I think he sees this whole damned place as nothing more than a hideously dangerous freak show, full of things that bite. He'd nuke the Nightside and wipe us all out, if he thought he could get away with it. Except he can't, because his mysterious masters won't let him. Because they, and those like them, need somewhere to come and play the games they can't play anywhere else, to wallow in the awful pleasures they can't even admit to in the everyday world.

"This is Walker, Joanna. Don't trust him."

"How very unkind," Walker murmured. He pulled up another chair and sat down at our table, exactly half-way between Joanna and me. He crossed his legs elegantly and laced his fingers together on the table before him. All around us conversations were starting up again, as it became clear Walker hadn't come for any of them. He leaned forward across the table, and despite myself I leaned forward a little too, to hear what he had to say. If Walker had taken an interest in me and my case, the situation had to be even more serious than I thought.

"People have been disappearing on Blaiston Street for some time now," Walker said briskly. "It took us a while to realise this, because they were the kind of people no-one misses. The homeless, the beggars, the drunks and drug-users. All the usual street trash. And even after the situation became clear, I saw no reason to become involved. Because, after all, no-one cared. Or at least, no-one who mattered. If anything, the area actually seemed to improve, for a while. By definition, anyone who ends up on Blaiston Street by choice has already opted out of the human race. But just recently . . . a number of rather important people have walked into Blaiston Street, and never come out again. So the word has come down from Above for me to investigate."

"Hold everything." I gave Walker my best hard look. "Just what would these *rather important people* have been doing in a cesspit like Blaiston Street?"

"Quite," said Walker. If my hard look was bothering him, he hid it very well. "None of them had any business being there. Blaiston Street has none of the usual attractions or temptations that might lead a normally sensible person to go slumming. It seems much more likely they were called, or possibly even summoned, there, by forces or individuals unknown. Except . . . if something that powerful had come into the Nightside, we should have detected its presence long before now. Unless it's hiding from us. Which, strictly speaking, is supposed to be impossible. So, a mystery. And you know how much I hate mysteries, Taylor. I was considering what to do for the best when I learned you'd reappeared in the Nightside; and then everything just fell into place. I understand you're tracking a runaway."

"This lady's daughter," I said. Walker inclined his head to Joanna again.

"And your gift leads you to believe she's in Blaiston Street?"

"Yes."

"And you have reason to believe she was called there?"

"Not necessarily against her will."

Walker made a vague dismissive gesture with one elegant hand. "Then you have twelve hours, Taylor, to discover the secrets of Blaiston Street and do whatever is necessary to re-establish the status quo. Should you fail, I will have no choice but to fall back on my original plan, and destroy the whole damned street, and everything in it, now and forever."

"You can't do that!" said Joanna. "Not while my Cathy's still in there!"

"Oh yes he can," I said. "He's done it before. Walker's always been a great admirer of the scorched earth option. And it wouldn't bother him in the least if he had to sacrifice a few innocents along the way.

Walker doesn't believe anyone's innocent. Plus, by involving me he doesn't have to put one of his own people at risk."

"Exactly," said Walker. He rose gracefully to his feet, checking the time on an old-fashioned gold fob watch from his waistcoat pocket. "Twelve hours, Taylor, and not a minute more." He put the watch away and looked at me thoughtfully. "A final warning. Remember . . . that nothing is ever what it seems, in the Nightside. I'd hate to think you've been away so long that you've forgotten such a basic fact of life here."

He hesitated, and for a moment I thought he might be about to say something more, but then our waitress came trotting back with my freshly laundered trench coat, and the moment passed. Walker smiled tolerantly as the waitress displayed the spotless coat for my approval.

"Very nice, Taylor. Very retro. I must be off now, about my business. So much to do, and so many to be doing it to. Welcome back, Taylor. Don't screw up."

He was already turning away to leave when I stopped him with my voice. "Walker, you were my father's friend."

He looked back at me. "Yes, John, I was."

"Did you ever find out what my mother was?"

"No," he said. "I never did. But if I ever do find her, I'll make her tell me. Before I kill her."

He smiled briefly, touched his fingertips to the

brim of his bowler hat, and left the café. No-one actually watched him go, but the general murmur of voices rose significantly once the door was safely shut behind him.

"Just what is it with you and him?" Joanna said finally. "Why did you let him talk to you like that?"

"Walker? Hell, I'd let him shit on my shoes if he wanted to."

"I haven't seen you back down to anyone since we got here," said Joanna. "What makes him so special?"

"Walker's different," I said. "Everyone gives Walker plenty of space. Not for who he is, but for what he represents."

"The Authorities?"

"Got it in one. Some questions are all the scarier for having no answer."

"But who watches the watchmen?" said Joanna. "Who keeps the Authorities honest?"

"We are drifting into decidedly murky philosophical waters," I said. "And we really don't have the time. Finish your nice Coke, and we'll go pay Blaiston Street a visit."

"About time!" said Joanna. And she gulped down the last of her icy Coke so fast it must have given her a headache.

NINE

A House on Blaiston Street

Blaiston Street butts onto the back end of nowhere. Shabby houses on a shabby street, where all the street-lights have been smashed, because the inhabitants feel more at home in the dark. Perhaps so they won't have to see how far they've fallen. I could practically feel the rats running for cover as I led Joanna down the street, but otherwise it was almost unnaturally still and quiet. Litter was piled everywhere in great festering heaps, and every inch of the dirty stone walls was covered in obscene graffiti. The whole place stank of decay—material, emotional and spiritual. All down the street, windows were missing, patched up with cardboard or paper or nothing at all.

Filth everywhere, from animals marking their territory, or from people who just didn't care any more. The houses were two rows of ancient tenements, neglected and despised, that would probably have fallen down if they hadn't been propping each other up.

Maybe Walker was right. A good bomb here could do millions of pounds of civic improvements.

And yet . . . something was wrong here. More than usually wrong. The street was strangely empty, deserted, abandoned. There were no homeless huddled in doorways, or under sagging fire-escapes. No beggars or muggers, no desperate souls looking to buy or sell; not even a single pale face peering from a window. Blaiston Street usually seethed with life like maggots in an open wound. I could hear the sounds of traffic and people from adjoining streets, but the sound was muted, strangely far away, as though from another world.

"Where the hell is everybody?" said Joanna quietly.

"Good question," I said. "And I don't think we're going to like the answer, when we find it. I'd like to think everyone just ran away, but . . . I'm beginning to suspect they weren't that lucky. I don't think anyone here got out alive. Something bad happened here. And it's still happening."

Joanna looked around her, and shuddered. "What in sweet Jesus' name could have summoned Cathy to a place like this?"

"Let's find out," I said, and calling up my gift I opened my private eye again. My gift was getting weaker, and so was I, but I was so close now it was just strong enough to show me Cathy's ghost prancing down the street, lit up from within by her own blazing emotions. I'd never seen anyone look so happy. She came to one particular house, that looked no different from any of the others, and stopped before it, studying it with solemn, child-wide eyes. The door opened slowly before her, and she ran up the stone steps and disappeared into the darkness beyond the door, smiling widely all the time, as though she was going to the best party in all the world. The door closed behind her, and that was that. I'd come to the end of the trail. For whatever reason, she'd never left that house again. I took Joanna by the hand and replayed the ghost so she could see it too.

"We've found her!" said Joanna, her hand clamping down on mine so hard it hurt. "She's here!"

"She was here," I said, pulling my hand free. "Let me check the house out before we go any further, see what my gift can tell us about the house's past and present occupants."

We walked right up to the house, and stopped at the foot of the dirty stone steps that led up to the paint-peeling door. Old bricks and mortar, smeared windows, and no signs of life anywhere. The door looked flimsy enough. I didn't think it could keep me out if I decided I wanted in, but this was the Night-

side, so you never knew . . . I raised my gift and concentrated on the house, and despite myself I made a
sudden, startled sound. There was no house before
me. No history, no emotions, no memories, not even
a simple sense of presence. As far as my gift was
concerned, I was standing before a vacant lot. There
was no house here, and never had been.

I grabbed Joanna's hand again, so she could see
what I wasn't seeing, and she jumped too.

"I don't understand. Where did the house go?"

"It didn't go anywhere," I said. "As far as I can
tell, there's never been any kind of house here."

I let go her hand and dropped my gift, and there
was the house again, right in front of me. Large as
life and twice as ugly.

"Is it another ghost?" said Joanna. "Like the
café?"

"No. I'd recognise that. This is solid. It has a
physical presence. We saw Cathy go into it. Something here . . . is playing games with us. Disguising
its true nature."

"Something inside the house?"

"Presumably. Which means the only way we're
going to get any answers is to force our way in, and
see for ourselves. A house . . . that isn't just a house.
I wonder what it is?"

"I don't give a damn what it is," Joanna said hotly.
"All that matters is finding my Cathy, and getting her
the hell out of here."

I grabbed her by the arm to stop her from charging up the steps. Her face was flushed with emotion at coming so close to the end of the chase, and her arm trembled under my hand. She looked at me angrily as I stopped her, and I made myself speak calmly and soothingly.

"We can't help Cathy by plunging headlong into traps. I don't believe in charging blindly into strange situations."

"Just as well I'm here then, isn't it?" said Suzie Shooter.

I looked round sharply, and there she was in the street behind me; Shotgun Suzie, smiling just a little smugly, the stock of her holstered pump-action shotgun peering at me over her leather-clad shoulder. I gave her my best glare.

"First Walker, and now you. I can remember when people weren't able to sneak up on me all the time."

"Getting old, Taylor," said Suzie. "Getting soft. Found anything for me to shoot yet?"

"Maybe," I said. I gestured at the house before us. "Our runaway is in there. Only my gift says there's something decidedly unnatural about this place."

Suzie sniffed. "Doesn't look like much. Let's do it. I'll lead the way, if you're worried."

"Not this time, Suzie," I said. "I have a really bad feeling about this house."

"You're always having bad feelings."

"And I'm usually right."

"True."

I made my way slowly up the stone steps. There still wasn't anyone around, but I could feel the pressure of watching eyes. Suzie moved in beside me like I'd never been away, like she belonged there, her shotgun already in her hands. Joanna brought up the rear, looking a little upset at being pushed into the background by Suzie's presence. The sound of our feet on the stone steps seemed unusually loud and carrying, but it didn't matter. Whatever was waiting for us inside the house that wasn't just a house, it knew we were there. I stopped before the door. There was no bell. No knocker or letter-box, either. I rapped on the door with my fist, and the wood seemed to give slightly under each blow, as though it was rotten. The sound of my knocking was eerily soft, muffled. There was no response from within.

"Want me to blow the lock out?" said Suzie.

I tried the door-handle, and it turned easily in my grasp. The discoloured metal of the door-knob was unpleasantly warm and moist to the touch. I rubbed my hand roughly on the side of my coat, and pushed the door open with the tip of my shoe. It fell back easily. Inside, there was only an impenetrable darkness, and not a sound anywhere. Joanna pushed in beside me, staring eagerly into the dark. She opened her mouth as though to call out to Cathy, but I stopped her. She glared at me again. There was an urgency in her now. I could feel it. Suzie produced a flashlight from some hidden pocket, turned it on and handed it to me. I nodded my thanks, and played the bright beam back and forth across the hallway before me. Hardly anything showed outside the beam, but the hall seemed long and wide and empty. I moved slowly forward, and Joanna and Suzie came with me.

Once we were safely inside, the door closed behind us if its own volition, and none of us were a bit surprised.

TEN

In the Belly of the Beast

The house was dark and empty, utterly quiet and almost unnaturally still. It was like walking into a hole in the world. It felt like something was holding its breath, while it waited to see what we would do next. My back and stomach muscles tensed as I walked slowly down the wide hallway, anticipating an attack that somehow never came. There was danger all around me, but I couldn't put a name to it, couldn't even tell what direction it might come from. I hadn't felt this nervous in the future Timeslip. But some traps you just have to walk into to get to where you're going.

Shadows danced jerkily around me as I played the

beam of my flashlight back and forth. For all its brightness, the beam didn't make much of an impression on the dark. I could make out the hall before me, two doors leading off to the right, and a stairway to my left that led up to the next floor. Ordinary, everyday sights made somehow sinister by the atmosphere they were generating. This was not a healthy place. Not for three small humans, wandering blindly in the dark. The air was thick and oppressive, hot and moist, like the artificial heat of a greenhouse, where great fleshy things are forced into life that could not normally survive. Suzie moved silently along beside me, glaring about her. She hefted her shotgun and sniffed heavily.

"Damp in here. Like the tropics. And the smell . . . I think it's decay . . ."

"It's an old place," I said. "No-one's looked after it in years."

"Not that kind of decay. Smells more like . . . rotting meat."

We exchanged a look, and then carried on down the hallway. Our slow footsteps echoed hollowly back from the bare plaster walls. No furniture, no fittings; no carpets or comforts of any kind. No decorations, no posters or paintings or even calendars on the walls. Nothing to show that anyone had ever lived here. That thought seemed significant, though I couldn't for the moment see how. We were, after all, in Blaiston Street. This wasn't a place where people came to live like people . . .

"Have you noticed the floor?" Suzie said quietly.

"What in particular?" I said.

"It's sticky."

"Oh, thanks a bunch," said Joanna. "I really didn't need to know that, thank you. The moment I get out of here I'm going to have to burn my shoes. This whole place is *diseased.*"

She was right back at my side again, staring almost twitchily about her. But she seemed more . . . impatient, than anything else. She didn't like the house, but it was clear the setting wasn't disturbing her anywhere near as much as it was getting to Suzie and me. Which was . . . curious. I assumed being this close to finding Cathy at last had driven all other thoughts aside. We stopped in the middle of the hall and looked around us. Suzie lowered her shotgun a little, having no-one to point it at.

"Looks like the last occupants of this dump did a moonlight flit, and took everything with them that wasn't actually nailed down."

I just nodded. I didn't trust myself to say anything sane and sensible, for the moment. I was feeling increasingly jumpy. There was an overwhelming sense of being watched, by unseen, unfriendly eyes. I kept wanting to look back over my shoulder, convinced I'd find something awful crouching there, waiting to spring; but I didn't. There was no-one there. Suzie would have known. And you don't last long in the Nightside if you can't learn to control your own instincts.

A mirror on the wall beside me caught my attention. It took me a moment to figure out what was wrong with it. The mirror wasn't showing any reflection. It was just a piece of clear glass in a wooden frame. It wasn't a mirror at all.

There were two doors to my right, leading to rooms beyond. Ordinary, unremarkable doors. I moved slowly over to the nearest, and immediately Suzie was right there with me, shotgun at the ready. Joanna hung back a little. I listened carefully at the first door, but all I could hear was my own breathing. I turned the handle slowly. It was wet in my hand, dripping moisture, like it was sweating from the heat. I wiped my palm on the side of my coat, and then pushed the door open. *Come into my parlour, said the spider to the fly.*

The door swung easily open. The hinges didn't make a sound. The room beyond was completely dark. I stayed just inside the doorway and flashed my light around the room. The darkness seemed to suck up the light. Still no furnishings or fittings, no personal signs or touches. It looked more like a film set than anything someone might call home. I stepped back into the hall and moved down to the next door. The second room was just like the first.

"Whatever was going on here, I think we missed

it," said Suzie. "Someone must have told them I was coming."

"No," I said. "That's not it. Something's still here. It's just hiding from us."

I walked over to the foot of the staircase. Bare wooden boards, simple banisters. No frills or fancies. No scuff marks or traces of wear, either. It could have been old or new or anything in between. Almost as though untouched by humans hands . . . I raised my voice in a carrying call.

"Hello! Anybody home?"

The close air flattened my voice, making it sound small and weak. And then from somewhere up on the next floor came the sound of a single door, slamming shut. Suzie and Joanna moved quickly over to join me at the foot of the stairs. And the door banged shut again, and again, and again. There was a horrid deliberateness to the sound, almost taunting, an open violence that was both a threat and an invitation. *Come up and see, if you dare.* I put my foot on the first step, and the banging door stopped immediately. Somehow, it knew. I looked at Suzie, and then at Joanna.

"Someone's home."

Joanna surged forward, and would have gone running blindly up the stairs, if I hadn't grabbed her by the arm and made her stop. She pulled fiercely away, fighting to be free, not even looking back at me, and I had to use all my strength to hang on to her. I said her name over and over, increasingly loudly, until finally she spun on me, breathing hard. Her face was hot and red and angry, almost furious.

"Let go of me, you bastard! Cathy's up there! I can feel it!"

"Joanna, we don't know *what*'s up there . . ."

"I know! I have to go to her, she needs me! Let go of my arm, you . . ."

When she found she couldn't pull or twist her arm out of my grasp, Joanna went for my face with her other hand. Her fingers were like claws. Suzie interrupted the blow easily, catching Joanna's wrist in a grip so hard it had to hurt her. Joanna snarled, and fought against her. Suzie applied pressure, forcing the wrist back against itself, and Joanna gasped, and stopped struggling. She glared at Suzie, who looked coldly back at her.

"No-one gets to hit John but me, Mrs. Barrett. Now behave yourself; or you can listen to the bones in your wrist breaking, one by one."

"Easy, Suzie," I said. "She's new to the Nightside. She doesn't understand the kind of dangers we could be facing."

Except she should have known, by now.

"Then she'd better learn fast," said Suzie. "I won't have her putting us at risk. I'll kill her myself first."

"Dead clients don't pay their bills," I reminded her.

Suzie sniffed and let go of Joanna's wrist, though

she pointedly stayed where she was, ready to intervene again, if necessary. I released Joanna's arm. She scowled at both of us, rubbing sulkily at her throbbing wrist. I tried really hard to sound calm and reasonable.

"You mustn't lose it now, Joanna. Not when we're this close. You've trusted me this far; trust me now to know what I'm doing. There could be anything at all up there, apart from Cathy, just waiting for us to walk into some cleverly set trap. We do this slowly and carefully, or we don't do it at all. Understood?"

Her mouth was a sulky pout, her eyes bright and almost viciously angry. "You don't understand what I'm feeling. You know nothing about a mother's love. She's up there. She needs me. I have to go to her!"

"Either you control yourself, or I'll have Suzie drag you back to the front door and kick your arse out onto the street," I said steadily. "For your own protection. I mean it, Joanna. The way you're acting now, you're not just a liability, you're a danger to us all. I know this place is . . . upsetting, but you can't let it get to you like this. This isn't like you, Joanna. You know it isn't."

"You don't know me at all, John," said Joanna, but her voice was markedly calmer. "I'm sorry. I'll behave. It's just . . . being this close is driving me crazy. Cathy's in trouble. I can feel it. I have to go to her. Let me stay, John. I'll be good, I promise."

That wasn't like Joanna either, but I nodded reluctantly, putting it all down to the influence the house was having on her. I was born in the Nightside, and this damned house was already playing games with my head. I made Joanna take several deep breaths, and it seemed to help her. I didn't like the effect the house was having on her. This frantic, almost out of control Joanna, wasn't at all the woman I'd come to know, and care for. She hadn't been this freaked out before, even in the Timeslip. It had to be the house.

"You shouldn't have brought her here, John," said Suzie. "She doesn't belong here."

Her voice wasn't especially harsh, or unforgiving. She was speaking the truth as she saw it, just as she always did.

Joanna glared at her, her voice rising angrily again. "You don't give a damn about what might have happened to my daughter! You're only here because I'm paying you to be here!"

"Damn right," said Suzie, entirely unmoved. "And you'd better be good for the money."

They went on snarling at each other for a while, in their own hot and cold way, but I wasn't really paying attention. The house, what there was of it, baffled me. I kept thinking I was missing something. Something had called, or even summoned, Cathy to this place, and all those missing *important people* Walker had mentioned, but now I was here, at the heart of the mystery, *there was nothing here*. Except for whatever was playing games up on the next floor. Nothing in the house, nothing at all . . . I started up the stairs, and Joanna and Suzie immediately stopped arguing and hurried after me, Suzie pushing forward to take her place at my side again, shotgun to the fore.

No more slamming doors. No reaction at all. When we got to the next floor, all we found were more bare walls and more doors leading off. All the doors were safely, securely, closed. Suzie looked slowly about her, checking for targets, the shotgun tracking along with her gaze. Joanna was all but trembling with eagerness, and I took a few seconds to impress on her that Suzie and I were going to take the point. I looked at the closed doors, and they looked smugly back at me. Suzie raised her voice suddenly.

"Is it me, or is it lighter up here?"

I frowned, as I realised I could make out much more on this floor, even outside of the flashlight's beam. "It's not you, Suzie. The gloom seems to be lifting; though I'm damned if I can see where the light's coming from . . ." I broke off, as I looked up at the ceiling and realised for the first time that there were no light bulbs, or even any sign of the original light fittings. Which was . . . unusual, even for Blaiston Street.

"I just had another thought," said Suzie. "And a rather unsettling one, at that. If this house isn't really here, what are we standing on, right now? Are we actually floating in mid air, over some vacant lot?"

"You're right," I said. "That is an unsettling thought. Just what I needed right now. Hang about while I check it out."

But when I went to raise my gift, nothing happened. Something from outside had wrapped itself around my head, unfelt but immovable, forcibly preventing me from opening my private eye, from seeing the world as it really was. I struggled against it, with what strength I had left, but there was nothing there that I could get a grip on. I swore briefly. What was going on here, that Something didn't want me to see, to understand? Suzie scowled about her, desperate for something solid she could attack.

"What do you want to do, John? Kick in all the doors and take it room by room? Shoot anything that moves and isn't the runaway?"

I gestured abruptly for her to be quiet, straining my ears for the sound I thought I'd caught. It was there, faint but definite. Not too far away, behind one of the closed doors; someone was giggling. Like a child with a secret. I padded quickly down the corridor, Joanna and Suzie right on my heels, stopping to listen at each door until I'd found the right one. I tried the handle, and it turned easily in my grasp, like an invitation. I pushed the door in an inch, and then stepped back. I gestured for Joanna to stick close to me, and then nodded to Suzie. She grinned briefly, kicked the door in, and we all surged forward into the room beyond.

It was bare and empty like the rest of the house, except for Cathy Barrett, found at last, lying flat on her back on a bare wooden floor on the other side of the room, covered from neck to toe by a long grubby raincoat, tucked under her chin like a blanket. She made no move to rise as her would-be rescuers charged in, just smiled happily at us as though she didn't have a care in the world.

"Hello," she said. "Come in. We've been expecting you."

I looked carefully about me, but there was no-one else in the room with her. I didn't discount the *we*, though. The continuing sense of an unseen watching presence was stronger than ever here. The light was brighter too, though there was still no obvious source for it. The more I studied the room, the more disturbing it felt. The room had no window, no contents, no details. Just walls and a floor and a ceiling. A sketch of a room. It was as though the house felt it didn't have to pretend any more, now that we'd come this far. I put away the flashlight and took a firm hold on Joanna's arm, to make sure she stayed with me. She didn't even seem to notice, all her attention fixed on her daughter, who hadn't even tried to raise up on one elbow to look at us more easily. I began to wonder if she could move.

Her gaunt face smiled equally at all of us, peering

over the collar of the raincoat. I almost didn't recognise her. She'd lost a hell of a lot of weight since the photo Joanna had shown me, back in my office, in another world. The bones of her face pressed out against taut, grey skin, and her once golden hair hung down across her hollowed features in dark greasy strings. She looked half-starved, her great eyes sunk right back into the sockets. In fact, she looked like she hadn't eaten properly in months, not just the few weeks she was supposed to have been missing. I glanced at Joanna, wondering if I should have been quite so ready to believe everything she'd told me. But no; that wasn't it. My gift had shown me Cathy entering this house only a few days ago, and she'd looked nothing like this then.

Suzie glared about her, the pump-action shotgun steady in her hands. "This stinks, John. Something's very wrong here."

"I know," I said. "I can feel it. It's the house."

"It's her!" said Joanna. "My Cathy. She's here!"

"She's not the only one here," I said. "Suzie, keep an eye on Joanna. Don't let her do anything silly."

I moved slowly forwards and knelt beside Cathy. The wooden floor seemed to give slightly under my weight. Cathy smiled happily at me, as though there was nowhere else in the world she'd rather be. Up close, she smelled *bad*, as though she'd been sick for weeks.

"Hello, Cathy," I said. "Your mother asked me to come and find you."

She considered this for a moment, still smiling her awful smile. "Why?"

"She was worried about you."

"She never was before." Her voice was calm but empty, as though she was remembering something that had happened a long time ago. "She had her business and her money and her boyfriends . . . She never needed me. I just got in the way. I'm free now. I'm happy here. I've got everything I ever wanted."

I didn't look around the empty room. "Cathy, we've come to take you out of here. Take you home."

"I am home," said Cathy, smiling her interminable smile. "And you're not taking me anywhere. The house won't let you."

And I fell screaming to the floor as something huge and dark and ravenously hungry smashed its way into my mind, revealing itself at last.

It hit me from all sides at once, tearing through my defences like they weren't even there. It was the house, and it was alive. Once it had looked like something else, and might again, but for now it was a house. And it was feeding.

Inch by inch I forced it out of my mind, my shields re-forming one by one until my thoughts were my own again, the house was gone, and the only one in my head was me. The effort alone would probably have killed anyone else. I came to myself again lying curled up on the bare floor beside Cathy, shaking and shuddering. A vicious headache beat in my temples, and blood was dripping steadily from my nose. Suzie was kneeling beside me, one hand on my shoulder, shouting something, but I couldn't hear her. Joanna was watching from the doorway, her face completely blank. With my cheek pressed against the bare wood of the floor, I slowly realised how warm it was. Warm and sweaty and curiously smooth. Deep within the pale wood, I could feel a faint pulsing.

I struggled up onto my hands and knees, Suzie helping me as best she could. Blood dripped onto the floor from my nose. I watched almost emotionlessly as the pale wood soaked up the blood, until there was no trace of it left. I knew what was happening now. I knew just what kind of trap I'd walked into. I reached out and pulled Cathy's coat away from her, revealing the truth. Naked and horribly emaciated, Cathy's body was slowly melting into the wooden floor. Already I could no longer tell where her flesh ended, and the floor's began.

ELEVEN

All Masks Thrown Aside

"It's the house," I said. "It's alive. And it's hungry."

I could feel the house all around me now, pulsing with alien life, roaring triumphantly at the edges of my mind. Laughing at me, now it didn't have to hide any more. I looked up and there was Suzie, breathing harshly, her knuckles showing white as she clung to her gun, the only thing that had always made sense to her. Her eyes darted wildly round the room, as she searched desperately for something she could hit or shoot. Joanna was standing very still by the doorway, not looking at Cathy. Her pale face was completely without expression, and when her gaze briefly crossed mine, I might as well have been a stranger. I looked back at Cathy.

"Tell me," I said. "Tell me why, Cathy. Why did you come here, to this place, of your own free will?"

"The house called me," she said happily. "It opened up a door, and I stepped through, and found myself in a whole new world. So bright and vivid; so *alive*. Like a movie going from black and white to colour. The house . . . needed me. I'd never felt needed before. It felt so good. And so I came here, and gave myself to the house, and now . . . I don't have to care about anything any more. The house made me happy, for the first time in my life. It loves me. It'll love you too."

I wiped the blood from my nose on the back of my hand, leaving a long crimson smear. "It's eating you, Cathy. The house is swallowing you up."

"I know," she said blissfully. "Isn't it wonderful? It's going to make me a part of it. Make me part of something greater, something more important than I could ever have been on my own. And I'll never have to feel bad again, never feel lost or alone or unhappy. Never have to worry about anything, ever again."

"That's because you'll be dead! It's lying to you, Cathy. Telling you what you want to hear. When the house attacked my mind, I was able to see it clearly at last, see it for what it really is. It's hungry. That's all it ever is. And you're just food, like all the other victims it's absorbed."

Cathy smiled at me, dying by inches and not caring, because the house wouldn't let her care. Suzie moved in beside me and hauled me bodily to my feet. She held me upright by brute strength until my legs stabilised again, and stuck her face right into mine.

"Talk to me, John! What's happening here? What is this house, really?"

I took a deep breath. It didn't steady me nearly as much as I'd hoped, but at least the shakes were starting to wear off now. Like so many times before in the Nightside, I had found the truth at last, and it didn't please or comfort me one bit.

"The house is a predator," I said. "An alien thing, from some alien place, far outside our own space, where life has taken very different forms. It makes itself into what it needs to be, taking on the colour of its surroundings, hiding in plain sight, calling its prey to it with a voice that cannot be resisted. Its prey is the lost and the lonely, the unloved and the uncared for, the discarded flotsam and jetsam of the city that no-one ever misses when it washes up here, on Blaiston Street. The house calls, in a voice that no-one ever disbelieves, because it tells them just what they want to hear. It even sucked in a few supposedly important people, people perhaps a little too susceptible for their own good. Being important doesn't necessarily protect you from the secret despairs of the hidden heart."

"Stick to the point, John," said Suzie, shaking me

by the shoulder. "The house lures people into it, and then?"

"And then it feeds on them," I said. "It sucks them dry, absorbing all they are into itself. It grows strong by feeding on their strength, keeping them happy while they last, so they won't try to escape. So they won't even want to."

"Jesus," said Suzie, looking down at Cathy's emaciated body. "From the look of the kid, the house has already taken most of her. Shame. We have to get out of here, John."

"What?" I said, not understanding, or perhaps not wanting to.

"There's nothing we can do," Suzie said flatly. "We got here too late. Even if we could maybe cut the kid free from the floor, odds are she'd bleed to death before we even got her to the street. She's already as good as dead. So we leave her, and get the hell out of here while we still can. Before the house turns on us."

I shook my head slowly. "I can't do that, Suzie. I can't just walk away and leave her here."

"Listen to me, John! I don't do lost causes. This case is *over*. All that's left to us is to give the kid a quick death, maybe cheat the house out of some of its victory. Then we get out of here, and come back with something heavy in the explosive line. You get Joanna moving. I'll take care of the kid."

"I didn't come all this way, just to abandon her! She's coming back with us!"

"No-one's leaving," said Cathy. "No-one's going anywhere."

Behind us, the door groaned loudly in its frame. Suzie and I looked round sharply, just in time to see the door slam shut and then vanish, its edges absorbed into the surrounding wall. The door's colours faded out, and within moments there was only an unmarked, unbroken expanse of wall, with no sign to show there'd ever been a door there. And all around us, the four walls of the enclosed room *rippled* suddenly, expanding and contracting in slow sluggish movements; becoming steadily more organic in appearance, soft and puffy and malleable. Thick purple traceries of veins spread across the walls, pulsing rhythmically. And a great inhuman eye opened in the ceiling above us, cold and alien, staring unblinkingly down at its new victims like some ancient and unsympathetic god. A sickly phosphorescent glow blazed from the walls, and I finally knew where the light had been coming from all along. There was a new smell on the air, thick and heavy, of blood and iron and caustic chemicals.

"No-one's going anywhere," said Cathy. "There's nowhere to go." There was another voice under hers now, harsh and deliberate and utterly inhuman.

Suzie stalked over to where the door had been, reversed her gun and slammed the butt of the shotgun against the wall. The awful pulsing surface gave a little under the blow, but it didn't break or even crack. Suzie hit it again and again, grunting with the effort she put into it, to no avail. She glared at the wall, breathing hard, and then kicked it in frustration. The leather toe of her boot clung stickily to the wall, and she had to use all her strength to pull it free. Part of the leather toe was missing, already absorbed. Drops of dark liquid fell from the ceiling, and more slid slowly down the walls and oozed up out of the floor. Suzie hissed suddenly, in surprise as much as pain, as a drop fell on her bare hand, and steam rose up from the scorched flesh.

"John, what the hell is this? What's going on?"

"Digestive juices," I said. "We're in a stomach. The house has decided we're too dangerous to absorb slowly, like Cathy. It doesn't want to savour us. We're going to be soup. Suzie, make us an exit. Blast a hole right through that wall."

Suzie grinned fiercely. "I thought you'd never ask. Stand back. This could splatter."

She trained her shotgun on the wall where the door had been, and let fly. The wall absorbed the blast, the point-blank impact producing only ripples spreading slowly outwards, like when you throw a stone into a pond. Suzie swore briefly and tried again, reloading and firing repeatedly till the close air stank of cordite, and the sound was overwhelming. But even as the roar of the gun died away, the ripples were already disappearing from the unmarked wall. Suzie looked back at me.

"We are in serious trouble, John. And don't look now, but your shoes are steaming."

"Of course," I said. "The house isn't fussy about what it eats."

Suzie looked at me steadily, waiting. Without an enemy she could hit or shoot, she was pretty much lost for another option; but she trusted me to find a way out of this mess. She'd always been too ready to trust me. That was one of the reasons why I'd left the Nightside in the first place. I got tired of letting my friends down. I thought hard. There had to be a way out of this. I hadn't come back after all these years, fought my way through all the madness, just to die in an oversized stomach. I hadn't come back to fail again. I looked at Cathy, and then I looked at Joanna, still standing very still by the living wall. She hadn't said a word or moved an inch since the house revealed itself. Her face was eerily calm, her eyes unfocused. She hadn't even flinched when Suzie opened fire right next to her. Shock, I supposed, then.

"Joanna!" I said loudly. "Come over here and talk to your daughter. See if you can focus her mind on you, separate her from the house. I think I've got an idea on how to break her and us free, but I don't know what effect it might have on her . . . Joanna! Listen to me!"

She turned her head slowly to look at me, and

there was a slow horror forming in her eyes that made me want to look away.

"Why are you talking to her about me?" said Cathy.

"Because I need your mother's help in this," I said.

"But that's not my mother," said Cathy.

The words seemed to resonate endlessly in the quiet room, their sudden awful significance driving all other thoughts out of my head. It never even occurred to me to doubt Cathy's word. I could hear the truth in her voice, even if I didn't want to. So many little things that hadn't made sense suddenly came together, in one terrible moment of insight. Joanna looked at me, and there was nothing in her eyes but a calm, resigned sadness. All the vitality had gone out of her. As though she didn't have to pretend any more.

"I'm sorry, John," she said slowly. "But I think it's all over now. My purpose is over, now you're here. I think I did care for you . . . but I don't think I'm who I thought I was . . ." Her voice changed, and under it I heard the harsh alien voice that had briefly spoken through Cathy. "I'm just a Judas Goat, the perfect bait, designed and programmed specifically to lure you back into the Nightside, so that you could be . . . dealt with."

"Why?" I said, and my voice was little more than a whisper.

"The house was provided with all the necessary details—the exact kind of client, the exact kind of case, the exact kind of woman who would most appeal to you. Someone who would slip past all your defences, make you disregard all your instincts, and lead you unresisting to your doom. There never was a Joanna Barrett—only a role to play, a function to perform. But they made me too well, John; and for a time I actually forgot what I was. I thought I was a real woman, with real feelings. There's enough left of me to be sorry about what's going to happen to you . . . but not enough for me to stop it."

"Was none of what we had real?" I said.

"Only you were real, John. Only you."

"And all . . . this?" I said. "Was all this set up just for me? Was the house invited into the Nightside, allowed to hunt and feed and kill, just to get *me*? Why? I'd left the Nightside! I was no threat to anyone any more! Why bring me back now?"

"Ask your mother," said the thing with Joanna's voice. "It seems she's coming back. And you . . . are a loose thread that could unravel everything."

"Who did this?" I said. "Who's behind this?"

"Can't you guess?" said Joanna. And her face slowly melted away, leaving behind only the perfect blank mask of the Harrowing.

I think I cried out then; the sound of some small animal as the steel trap finally closes on it. Joanna leaned back into the living wall, and sank into it, the soft pulsing surface closing over her as the house re-absorbed the thing it had created, or birthed. In a moment she was gone, leaving only slow ripples behind, and soon they were gone too. I should have known. I should have remembered. You can't trust anyone, or anything, in the Nightside, to be what it appears to be. Walker had tried to warn me, but I didn't listen. I'd forgotten that here, love is just another weapon they can use to hurt you, and that the past never goes away. I felt the tears running down my cheek long before I knew I was crying.

"Damn," said Suzie, glowering at the wall Joanna had disappeared into. "Guess I'm not going to get paid for this one after all."

She looked at me, and sighed when I didn't react. The digestive juices were falling from the ceiling in a steady rain now, stinging and burning my bare face and hands, and I didn't care at all. Someone, or something, had just punched my heart out, and I didn't care about anything. Suzie came over and put a hand on my shoulder, staring right into my face. She wasn't very good with emotions, but she did her best.

"John, you have to listen to me. You can mourn her later. Whatever she was, or might have been. You can't fall apart now. We have to get out of here."

"Why?" I said. "Everyone wants me dead; and maybe I do too."

She slapped me across the face, more professionally than angrily. "What about me, John?"

"What about you?"

"All right, maybe I deserved that. I never should have let you go running off to hide in London. And I wasn't always the best of friends to you; I don't seem to have the knack. But what about the kid, John? Cathy? Remember her? The one you came back into the Nightside to save? Are you going to let her down now? Are you going to let her die, just because you're feeling sorry for yourself?"

I turned my head slowly, and looked at Cathy. What was left of her. "No," I said finally. "None of this is her fault. And I never let a client down. Take my hand, Suzie."

"What? This is no time to be getting sentimental, John."

I looked back at her. "You have to trust me on this, Suzie. Trust me to know what I'm doing. We can't fight our way out, so that just leaves me, and my gift."

Suzie looked at me for a long moment, reassuring herself that I was back in control again, and then nodded briskly. She slid her shotgun into the holster behind her shoulder and took my hand in hers. I could feel the calluses on her palm, but her grip was firm and steady. She had faith in me. Which made one of us. I sighed, tiredly, getting ready to fight the good fight one more time, because that was all I had left.

"We need to find the heart of the house," I said. "Kill the heart, and kill the house. But the heart won't be anywhere here. The house will have hidden it somewhere else, for protection. Somewhere . . . no-one would be able to reach it, normally. But then, I'm not normal. I can find it. I can find anything."

Except what matters most. I reached inside myself and summoned up my gift, opening my mind again. And the house pounced.

For a long time I was nowhere, and it felt good. Good not to have to worry about bills that needed paying, cases that couldn't be solved, clients who couldn't be helped. Good not to have to worry about all the mysteries of my life, and the endless pain they brought to me and those I cared for. When I started out I had a dream, a dream of helping people who had nowhere else to turn; but dreams don't last. They can't compete with reality. The reality of struggling to find money for food and rent, and the way your feet hurt from pounding the streets looking for people who don't want to be found.

The harsh, unyielding reality of having to compromise your ideals bit by bit, day by day, just to achieve a few little victories in the face of the world's malice, or indifference. Until sometimes you wonder if there's nothing left of you but the shell of the man you intended to be, just going through the motions because you've nothing better to do.

But somehow the dream doesn't quite die. Because in the Nightside, sometimes dreams are all that can keep you going. Give them up, and you're dead.

Growing up in the Nightside, I saw a lot of dead men walking about. They could walk and talk and go through the motions, drifting from bar to bar and from drink to drink, but there was nothing left behind their eyes. Nothing that mattered. My father was a dead man for years, long before his heart finally, mercifully, gave out, and they nailed the coffin lid down. I couldn't help him. I was only a kid.

My gift didn't kick in until much later. A gift I could use, to make a difference. For other people, if not myself.

In the safe nowhere nothing that surrounded and comforted me, gentle waves of love and affection lapped against my mind, wanting me to forget all that. To forget everything but an eternal now of love and happiness, an end to all wanting and needing, and a rest that would never end. A quiet murmuring voice promised me I could have everything I ever wanted; all I had to do was lie back and accept, and give up the fight. But I didn't believe the voice. Because the only thing I really wanted had already been taken from me, when the house took Joanna back into itself. The voice spoke more urgently, and I sneered at it. Because underneath the voice I could still hear the endless, insatiable hunger.

My dreams. My reality. I clung to them like a drowning man, and would not give them up. They made me what I am. Not the father who ignored me, or the mother who abandoned me. Not the mysterious inheritance I never wanted, and not even the faceless hordes who'd hounded me all my life. So many influences trying to shape me, and I disowned them all. I chose to help people, because there'd been no-one there to help me when I needed it. I knew even then that I couldn't trust the Authorities to save me. My father had been one of them, and they still hadn't been able to protect him, or comfort him. I shaped my own life, determined my own destiny; and to hell with everyone and everything else.

My anger was rising now, hot and fierce and strong, and it pushed back the false promises of love and happiness, perhaps because deep down I'd never believed in such things. Not for me, anyway. The empty nothingness was fragmenting, falling apart. I could sense other people around me. Suzie Shooter, a ghost hand in mine, quietly confident in me. Cathy Barrett, understanding for the first time just how much she'd been lied to, manipulated and abused, almost as angry as I was. And somewhere close at hand . . . a faint presence, a quiet voice, like the last echoes of someone who had briefly believed themselves to be a woman called Joanna. And I swear I felt another ghostly hand in mine.

I reached out and embraced them, binding them to me with my gift; and together we were stronger than any damned house.

I don't just find things with my gift. It can do other things too. Like identify an enemy's weak spot and attack it. I lashed out with my gift, and the house screamed, in shock and rage, pain and horror. I think it had been a very long time since anyone had been able to hurt it.

The nothing was replaced by something. An in-between place. I was standing on a bare plain that stretched out to infinity in all directions. It was a grey place, soft and hazy and indistinct. Not a real place, but real enough. A place to make a stand. Suzie and Cathy were there with me. Suzie was wearing silver armour, studded with vicious spikes. Cathy looked like she had in her old photo, only mad as hell now. I didn't look down to see how I appeared. It didn't matter. Not too far away there was another presence, too faint to be clearly seen, but I knew who it was. Who it had to be. We were all shining brightly now, luminous beings in a grey world. Together we formed a wide circle around a column of swirling darkness, shot with vivid blood-red traces, that towered endlessly up into the featureless sky. From it came the voice of the house, beating against us like hammer-blows, harsh and inhuman.

"Mine! Mine! Mine!"

But the gift was strong in me, and I just laughed at the voice. All it really had on its side was stealth and lies, and neither could serve the house here. I stepped forward, and Suzie and Cathy moved with me. The dark column actually shrank back from our light, shrinking and contracting away from us. We closed in, and the column became narrower. And all around us, on that wide and endless plain; hundreds and hundreds of insubstantial figures, standing silently, watching and hoping. All the house's victims. It hadn't just eaten their bodies; the damned thing had consumed their souls too, holding them within itself to power its unnatural existence. What was left of a woman called Joanna came forward, holding herself together despite everything the house could do to tear her apart and assimilate her, and again I felt her hand in mine. Through her I reached out to the other captive shades, silently offering them a chance for revenge, and the only freedom they could ever know now . . . and they reached out to me.

Power surged through me, igniting my gift, and I blazed so very brightly as I advanced on the dark column before me. Suzie and Cathy and all the other victims advanced with me, and the house screamed and screamed. The column shrank and compacted, growing thinner and thinner, until finally I was able to join my shining hands with the trusting Suzie, the furious and betrayed Cathy, and the ghost of a woman I could have loved. We were all shining like suns now. I gathered together all our rage and hate and need, channeling all the many victims through my gift, and struck out at the dark heart of the thing that pretended to be a house. It howled once, with impotent horror, and then the dark swirling column was suddenly gone, and the voice of the house was stilled forever.

The other side of my gift. To find another's death. I've never carried a gun. I don't need one.

I looked around the endless plain, that grey and empty place, and all the hundreds of victims were gone, their souls released at last to find the only peace left to them. And gone with them, a designed and programmed piece of bait that had briefly learned what it was to be human, and would not give it up.

You have to believe in dreams, because sometimes they believe in you.

I fell back into my body and glared wildly about me. All my strength was back, restored by the departed souls of the house's victims. I was still trapped in an enclosed room, with no way out, but the house was dead now. Already the air was thick with the sweet cloying stench of decay. The eye in the ceiling was closed and gone, and the phosphorescent glow from the walls was slowly fading. Ragged cracks spread slowly across the walls, tearing them apart like rotting flesh. And there, on the floor, what was left of Cathy Barrett. Gaunt, desiccated and half-dead, but finally separate from the consuming floor, ejected by the house's dying spasms, as I'd hoped. She was struggling to sit up, her face mad as hell. I helped her sit up, and wrapped the long coat around her. She held it closed with hands that were little more than bone and skin, and managed a brief, but real, smile for me.

"It lied to me," she said. "It told me everything I secretly wanted to hear, so I believed it. And when it finally had me, it made me happy; but inside I was screaming all the time. You saved me."

"It's what I do," I said. "It's my job."

She studied me for a while. "If my mother had known I was here, and in trouble, I like to think she would have sent someone like you. Someone . . . reliable."

"Look, this is all touching as hell," Suzie said briskly, "but I'd really like to get out of here."

"Good point," I said. "I've only just had this trench coat cleaned."

Together, we got Cathy onto her feet and helped support her. It wasn't difficult. She couldn't have weighed more than seventy pounds.

"Where were we?" she said abruptly. "The grey place. What was that?"

"The house was only vulnerable through its heart,"

I said, urging her towards the place in the wall where the door had been. "So, the house hid its heart in another place. Another dimension of reality, if you like. It's an old magical trick. But I can find anything."

"Are you sure it's dead?" said Suzie. "All the way, not coming back in the last reel, dead? I mean, it's still here, and we're still trapped inside it."

"It's dead," I said. "And from the smell and general state of things, I'd say its body is already starting to decay. It never really belonged in our world. Only its augmented will allowed it to survive here. Suzie, make us a door."

She looked at me. "You might remember, my gun didn't work too well, last time."

"I think you'll find it will now."

Suzie grinned like a child who's just been presented with an unexpected present, and drew her shotgun while I supported Cathy. Suzie opened fire on the wall at point-blank range again, and this time the blast punched a hole right through the wall, blowing it apart like rotten meat. Suzie loaded and fired again and again, laughing aloud as she widened the hole, and finally stepped forward to tear at the edges of the hole with her bare hands, widening it still further. She looked at the filth dripping from her hands, and grimaced.

"Damn stuff is falling apart."

"The whole house will fall apart soon," I said. "And lose what's left of its precarious hold on our reality. I really don't think we should be here when that happens; do you? Give me a hand here, Suzie."

We took a firm hold on Cathy's frail body and forced our way through the ragged gap in the wall, half-falling out onto the trembling corridor beyond. We'd barely got our feet under us before the edges of the hole in the wall behind us ran together like melting wax. Strange lights glowed everywhere, like the dim unhealthy glows of corpsefires, and the sickly-sweet stench of corruption was fast becoming overwhelming. I hurried us along the corridor towards the stairs, and the walls we passed were already developing black, diseased patches. The ceiling was bowing down towards our heads, as though it could no longer support itself. The whole floor was shuddering now, and the jagged cracks in the walls were lengthening in sudden spurts. By the time we got to the top of the stairs, the floor was sagging dangerously under our feet.

"Let's move like we have a purpose, people," I said. "I don't think this house is long for this world. And I really don't think we'd like being trapped in the kind of world that could produce a creature such as this."

"Right," said Suzie. "I'd have to kill everything in it, just on general principles. And I didn't bring enough ammunition with me."

We hurried down the swaying stairs, Cathy helping as best she could, which wasn't much. The house had eaten most of her muscles. She was still game as hell, though. The wall beside the stairs was melting slowly, like wax running down a candle. The steps clung to our feet like sticky toffee, until we had to drag them free by brute force. I grabbed at the banister for support, and a whole chunk of it came away in my hand, rotting and purulent. I pulled a face, and threw the stuff away.

We hit the wide hallway running, mostly carrying Cathy now, while the swaying walls bulged forwards on all sides, and the ceiling fell on us in thick muddy drops. Where the front door had been there was only a slumping, rotting hole, dark and purple, its edges dripping like a diseased wound. It was slowly irising shut, collapsing in on itself. Already it was far too small for any of us to get through.

"Oh God," said Cathy. "We're never going to get out of here. It's never going to let us go."

"It's dead," said Suzie. "It doesn't have a say in the matter. And we are leaving, whatever it takes. Right, Taylor?"

"Right," I said.

Beyond the collapsing hole that had once pretended to be a door, I could see a glimpse of the outside world, clear and calm and relatively sane. I glared at the closing hole, bludgeoning it with my gift, and it winced open, reluctantly widening again. Suzie and I took firm hold of Cathy and charged the hole, hitting it at a dead run. The decaying tissues grabbed at us, but we crashed through and out in a moment. We burst onto Blaiston Street, back into the world of men, and the newly falling rain washed us clean.

We staggered to a halt in the middle of the street, whooping like crazy in celebration, and lowered Cathy to the ground. She ran her hands over the solid street, that might have been filthy dirty but never pretended to be anything other than what it was, and started to cry. I looked back at the dead house. It was slowly sagging and falling in on itself, the windows drooping shut like so many tired eyes. What was left of the hole we'd crashed through looked like nothing more than a bruised, pouting mouth.

"Rot in hell," I said.

I hit the dead thing with my gift one last time, pushing it over the edge, and what was left of the creature that had pretended to be a house dropped out of the Nightside and was gone, back to whatever awful place it had come from, leaving behind only a few decaying chunks and a stench of corruption already slowly dissipating in the rain. By the time Walker arrived with his people, there wasn't even anything left to bury.

EPILOGUE

The rain had mostly died away. I was shaking just a little, probably not from the cold. At least the night sky was still packed with stars and a huge white moon, and I tried to take some comfort from that. I sat on the pavement, hunched inside my filthy trench coat, watching Walker's people on the other side of the road as they swarmed all over the vacant lot where the house had been. They didn't seem to be having much luck, but every now and again they'd get all excited over some mess of decaying tissue, and make a big deal about sealing it into a snap-lock plastic bag. For evidence, or later analysis, perhaps.

Or maybe Walker just fancied his chances of growing himself a new house. Walker was always on the look-out for some new dirty trick he could spring on whoever happened to be his enemy that week. He was currently ordering his people about from a very safe distance, careful as always not to get his own hands dirty.

He turned up with a small army of his people not long after I'd brought Suzie and Cathy out of the dead house. He and they had been standing by, observing, just in case I screwed up after all. Apparently Walker had heard the house scream as it died. I had no trouble believing that. I'd always thought Walker would make a really good vulture.

Cathy sat beside me, still wrapped in the long grubby coat she refused to give up, leaning companionably against me. Walker had conjured up a large mug of beef tea for her from somewhere, and she sipped at it now and again, when she remembered. Her body had been so reduced by the house it had even forgotten how to be hungry. Suzie stood guard over us with her shotgun in her hands, giving Walker the hard look if he even looked like drifting too close to us. Even Walker knew better than to cross Suzie Shooter unnecessarily.

The memory of Joanna still haunted me, though her ghost had disappeared along with the house. I couldn't believe she'd fooled me for so long . . . but she'd seemed so real. I had to wonder whether I'd believed in her for the same reasons that Cathy had believed the house's promises, because we were told just what we wanted to hear. That I'd loved Joanna because she'd been created specifically by my enemies to be my perfect love. Hard, but vulnerable. Strong, but desperate. A lot like me, in fact. Someone had done their homework very well, the bastards. But I still think that in the end Joanna believed in herself because I believed in her, that she became, if only briefly, a real person through an effort of will. Her own will. Dreams can come true, in the Nightside. Everyone knows that.

But they still vanish when you wake up.

Suzie looked down at me, frowning, correctly divining my thoughts. "You always were too soft for your own good, Taylor. You'll get over her. Hey, you still got me."

"Lucky me," I said. She meant well, in her own way.

"And we kicked that house's arse, didn't we?"

"Yes," I said. "We did that."

Suzie looked across at the vacant lot, unimpressed by Walker's people and their efforts. "How many people did that thing eat, do you think, before we shut it down?"

I shrugged. "How many lost souls and losers are there, in the Nightside? And how many of them would have to go missing, before anyone noticed? Or cared? Walker only got involved after a few movers and shakers accidentally got sucked in."

Walker picked up on his name, and strolled casually over to join us, keeping a wary eye on Suzie. She turned her gun on him, smiling unpleasantly, but I gestured for her to let him approach. There were things I needed to know, now I was feeling a little stronger. He tipped his bowler hat to us politely.

"You knew," I said.

"I suspected," said Walker.

"If you'd been sure," I said slowly, "would you still have let me go in there, not knowing?"

"Probably. You're not one of my people, Taylor. I don't owe you anything."

"Not even the truth?"

"Oh, especially not that."

Suzie frowned. "Are you two talking about the house, or Joanna?"

"It doesn't matter," I said. "Walker has always been very jealous of the secrets he guards. Tell me this, Walker. Is my mother really coming back?"

"I don't know," he said, holding my gaze calmly. His manner was open and sincere, but then, it always was. "There are rumours . . . but there are always rumours, aren't there? Perhaps . . . you should stick around, just in case." He looked across at the vacant lot, so he wouldn't have to look at me. "I could always put a little work your way, now and again. Unofficially, of course. Since it seems you haven't lost your touch, after all."

"You've got some nerve," said Suzie.

He smiled at her, every inch the polite and demure civil servant. "Comes with the job, my dear."

"I am not your dear, Walker."

"And don't think I'm not grateful."

I intervened, before things started getting out of hand. "Walker, can you look after Cathy for me? See that she gets back to the real world, and her mother? Her real mother?"

"Of course," said Walker.

"You can forget that shit," Cathy said sharply. "I'm not going back. I'm not ever going back. I'm staying here, in the Nightside."

I gave her my best harsh glare. "Are you crazy? After everything you've been through?"

She smiled at me over her mug of beef tea, and there wasn't a trace of humour in that smile. "There's more than one kind of nightmare. Trust me; bad as this place can be, it's still nothing compared to what I ran away from. I thought I'd stay with you, John. Could you use a secretary? Every private eye has to have a smart-mouthed secretary who knows a thing or two. I think it's in the rule book."

Suzie started to laugh, and then turned it into an unconvincing coughing fit when I glared at her. Walker became very interested in the vacant lot again. I glowered at Cathy.

"I just saved your life; I haven't adopted you!"

"We'll sort something out," Cathy said confidently. She looked across the road too. "What was it, do you think, really?"

"Just another predator," I said. "A little less obvious than most. Just . . . something from the Nightside."